EST. 199X

BY KJ ETIENNE

Est. 199X

Ki Etienne

ISBN: 0692371036
ISBN-13: 978-0-692-37103-9

Summary: A series of rants, revelations, and poetry about the realities of growing up in the modern world as told by an anonymous blogger known as "X"

Dedication

*To Bree Mae and Ochuole Ode for making me
excited about books again.
To my parents for letting me stay home to write this
one. I'm still not leaving. ;)
-Ki*

Table of Contents

Expectations and Intentions

Introductions are difficult when you have no intention of ever telling the person you're talking to your name, age, or even your gender. I hope you don't mind the secrecy, because it isn't anything personal. It's just that the stifled feelings that I need to express are too confidential to attach a shred of recognition from myself to these blog posts. Besides, you don't have to tell me your name or anything either.

I'm starting to believe that loneliness is the most common emotion of the human experience. Ironic, isn't it? There is technology in this world that allows us to touch someone else's heart even though we don't have the ability to physically touch their hand. We're able to reach across the world's time zones and have face to face conversations while one person is experiencing Tuesday, but Monday's Blues are raging on for the other.

We live in a place where there are countless ways to connect with other people, yet as a whole we feel more isolated than we ever have in human history. How is it that with home phones, cell phones, social media sites, and video calls consuming most of our free time, we are unable to stand in an elevator with a stranger and hold a brief conversation? Why is it that we have hundreds of "friends" on Facebook, but we never make an effort to see them in real life (or pretend not to notice them when we do)? I don't think there is a young adult in the United States who hasn't fled to the comfort of an electronic device in order to avoid speaking to someone.

While the disconnect that we've created through modern technology can be an obstacle to our happiness, I realize there is simultaneously a problem of everyone being too close to each other. There is almost nothing about a person that we don't know if we follow them on social media. We know when they wake up, when they go to the gym, when and what they are eating—we're sick of them before we ever talk to them personally.

We also see the things that they say to other people, and we learn their political views in great detail. It removes the human qualities that we'd experience in person, and allows us to judge only a small fragment of a person. The little quirks remain hidden while the parts that we don't like are blatantly obvious, so we begin to feel like there is no one in existence who sees the world remotely close to the way we do. The next thing we know, we're lonely, but we don't want to talk to anyone.

I think that every human has a need to spend some time alone, relishing in the comfort of knowing that there are no judgmental eyes within the nearby perimeters. I like to think of my mind as a group of four year olds who are sitting in a classroom for the first time. They arrive to class with excitement and try their best to behave according to the rules that the teacher has set, eager to bring the ultimate achievement of a gold star home to their parents. However, after hours of conforming to the rules, the desire to run and scream becomes overwhelming. Time begins passing too slowly, the walls start closing in, and suddenly there is no price imaginable that's too great in exchange for the ability to leave the classroom.

That's how I feel when I'm around people whom I don't know. As soon as I arrive to the classroom known as "the real world," sitting down becomes too difficult. I feel like every person in public is a teacher whom I have to behave for; otherwise, my parents will receive a disappointing phone call informing them that I'm unfit for the classroom, and my gold star will be taken away. My heart begins to race with anticipation, my limbs tingle with urgency, and there is nothing that I wouldn't give to be able to run out to the playground. I yearn for the much anticipated summer vacation that follows each school year, but there is no escaping this classroom because it's everywhere that I go.

I used to think that home was the safe haven that I would always be able to run to, but becoming a young adult and watching the simplicity of my childhood slip away has only served as a reminder that everything is temporary. My house and the people living in it will not be here forever. I won't always be able to flee into my room while someone else talks to my "teachers" for me. Eventually, I'll be expected to be in class every day, not as a student, but as the teacher. I'll be responsible for operating a classroom that I can hardly tolerate being in.

The pressure of having to meet the expectations that society has placed on me used to cause my knees to buckle, and leave me sprawled out on the floor in tears. I tried exhaustively to be everything that was expected of me, but every day I failed to bring home a gold star. Suddenly, one morning I woke up and didn't give a shit about a star—gold, red, green, or otherwise. I didn't care if the classroom remained intact. I didn't care if the foundation that it rested on was sturdy or not. If the entire campus fell through a crack in the Earth, or even if the Earth itself exploded—I wouldn't have given a single fuck.

I haven't cared about *almost* anything in the past 21 months. Yet somehow, despite being trapped behind the seemingly impenetrable walls of awkwardness, introverted tendencies, and confusion; there remains a very short list of things that transcend the depths of my apathy, and reside inside these walls with me. I exist with them wrapped safely at the core of my being.

This all inclusive list of "give a fuck" is composed of the following items:

1. Approximately five people, including my parents

2. Not *completely* screwing up my life
3. Figuring out what the hell is currently going on with my life, because I think I'm *completely* screwing it up.

The list of things that dwell with me behind the barriers can be counted on one hand, and I'd have two fingers left over. That realization always sends a spark of panic rushing along my spine. How in the world can a person only care about three things, two of which are ideas and not tangible things?

Becoming a young adult in today's world has left me constantly searching for something more than what has already been offered to me. I keep hoping to stumble upon something that's worth adding to that list of important things, but I can't find anything. Some people wish for a million dollars, or a mansion with an expensive car, but I just want to be able to use both of my hands when I count the shit that I care about. You don't know frustration until you're looking for something 24 hours a day, seven days a week, and you don't even know what the hell you're looking for. It feels like your next big break is right around the next corner, but you're living in a circle.

The only thing that seems to be able to explain why my list is so short is the last item on it, so that's what I've decided to focus on, figuring out my own path. This inner odyssey brought forth a slew of experiences that led me right back to the one thing that I've been doing since I was six—writing things down. Somewhere behind my bed is a box filled with pages of rants, meltdowns, poetry (but not the *real* kind), and insecurities that I could never share with anyone else.

Talking to others has never really been my strong point. I'm so bad at it that my doctors and school counselor gave it a name: Social anxiety. I absolutely loathe the fact that my mental composition has a mental illness named after it, but I'm also relieved by the fact that I'm not just super weird. I always hesitate to admit my diagnosis to anyone though, because I haven't found a person without it who remotely understands it. That would be perfectly fine if people accepted their ignorance, but they don't. Instead, they affix a stigma of being "lazy," or "attention seeking" to my condition.

The misunderstanding affects me twofold, because not only do they assume that I'm making all of this up, but they also assume that it is the focal point of my life, which couldn't be farther from the truth. They don't understand that if my life were a solar system, I would be the sun. I don't revolve around social anxiety. It revolves around me as a component of my total being. I am not social anxiety. I am thoughtful. I am curious. I am composed of moments of happiness, laughter, and excitement. I am laced with confusion, insecurity, and doubt. I enjoy a compliment just as much as the next person. No, social anxiety is not the focal point of my solar system. It's Venus; fairly close to the center, but ultimately a small segment of a much larger picture.

Writing is not what people think I should be doing with my allotted time in this life. It is presumed that it would be better spent working toward securing a position to work for someone else. They think that writing is just a coping mechanism that should have been put away with my childhood innocence. However, the beauty of not caring about almost anything is that those people don't worry me anymore, because they aren't included in the select group of individuals whom I mentioned earlier.

However, I do understand their point. I'm pretty sure there are just over a bajillion blogs in the world that are about the "realities" of being a young adult, and I'm only adding fuel to a fire that has been burning for far too long already. Stereotypically, I should go on about this moment in life being so pointless that I exist for nothing more than binge drinking, hooking up, and blacking out on the newest substances available, but I'm not going to do that because that's not what being a young adult is about for me.

I don't like alcohol. I don't hook up. The only drugs that I've taken have been prescribed to me due to anxiety. I don't smoke, and blacking out is not how I want to spend my life. What's the point in living if I can't remember what the hell I did while I was alive? There's no GPS on life. I know that I have to find my own way, but I'll never find it if I'm blackout drunk on someone's couch. Everyone's reality is different, and I want to share mine in the hopes that *someone* out there will understand it just a little bit.

I don't intend to change anyone's life with this blog. In fact, there are about 10,000 excuses that I came up with as to why I shouldn't write any of this down. Some of them are very valid reasons, but when I die I want to die on empty. I do not want my brain to rip at the seams with my thoughts, stories, poetry, and advice tangled up within me. The fact that I have social anxiety doesn't mean that I don't have anything to say, so I finally took my letters out of the metaphorical bottle and wrote them down in a safe place.

We're often told that we can't have our cake and eat it too, but when you're as lost as I am, you don't give a fuck about who eats the cake. You spend your days and nights just hoping that you don't burn the cake. Hell, some days you just hope that there *is* a cake. This blog is my version of a three-tiered chocolate and vanilla cake. I can't promise that you'll enjoy the taste of it, but you're welcomed to a slice any time.

-X

GROWING UP

Scavenger Hunt

I'll lay you in this space;
For now, it's your home.
Grow into it for about 9 months,
But then you must move along.

Things will get crazy,
And toss you heels over head,
But that's the way it should be,
It's for the best, truth be said.
You're to come down through the tunnel;
Your guardian will help you out.
She's given all she has to get you here,
So she's on your team, no doubt.

Enough about that,
Most people get there just fine.
Let's talk about what you're to do
Once you've arrived.

You've been equipped with a list
Of all the things that you need,
But listen to me carefully,
This is a warning you should heed.
The list that you have
Is not one you can see.

It's been written inside of you,
Knitted into your heart as it should be.

The task sounds quite simple,
Just find what's on a list,
But what you feel,
What you think,
And what you know
All coexist.

It is hard enough to practice love
Regardless of your emotions,
But wait until you try remembering what you know
Despite your brain's commotion.
Add the fact that the things you must find
Are not things you can touch.
You'll need courage, honesty, selflessness,
Determination, and such.

It tends to begin fairly easily,
Every item on the list will likely be crossed.
Then you'll begin "growing up,"
And a lot of what you found will be lost.

At age four you'll know exactly who you are.
Somehow, by age 13, the list of what you know is quite
        small.
The teenaged years are confusing,

Filled with tumbles and falls.
By the time you reach your 20's
You'll swear you know nothing at all!

People say it gets better by age 30,
But that's just what I've heard.
No one wants to age past the 20's,
So that sounds completely absurd.
As you grow older,
Some things get harder--like movement,
They say things just start breaking,
So what's the improvement?

You're probably getting scared.
Sorry if I've made it sound tough,
But there's no point in lying,
You'd find out soon enough.
The most important thing you must know
Is that you cannot cheat.
Everyone's list is quite different,
So there's no need to compete.

Many complete the tasks,
So there's hope, remember this.
But don't be too complacent,
Because some never even find the list.

Unwanted Advice

I know that there was a time in my life when I used to genuinely enjoy having company. I remember my heart used to flutter with excitement when someone knocked on the door unexpectedly, and an intense disappointment would rip through my chest when the visit was over. There was no greater sadness than watching everyone leave to return to their regularly scheduled lives, which seemed to take place too far away from my own. I don't know why I used to feel like that, but it's something that I haven't felt since approximately three hours after I hit puberty.

The only new factor that has entered the picture during this time, other than my own raging hormones, is unwanted advice. I cannot sneeze to the left without someone giving me their opinion about why I need to aim my mucus cannon in a different, better direction.

I get it, okay? I understand that most of these people mean well. I will go so far as to agree that I should be thankful that there are people in my life who want to steer me into the right direction. However, I need for all of these people to understand that I'd have to split my ass into a minimum of 17 pieces in order to go into all of the directions that everyone is pointing me toward.

I'm extremely confused by the fact that most of these individuals were spawned from the same family line as myself. I would have thought that a family would have similarities in what they believed about achieving things in life, but not my family. I have a group of cheerleaders for each option available to me as a young adult, and a few for options that are so far out of my reach that suggesting them is like telling me to walk on water.

The unwanted advice started off innocently enough when I was just a tween. It was a dangerously beautiful day outside, and my family decided to gather for a barbecue cookout. I put on my most comfortable pants because the only thing that I had on my mind was eating as much as I possibly could, then and partaking in that activity again as many times as possible without making myself sick and puking.

I was completely comfortable with my unkempt appearance; however, as soon as I stepped outside I was not greeted with a "hello" or anything remotely close to a warm, friendly welcome. No, the first comment I received was, "Wow, what happened to your skin?" The second was everyone's favorite thing to hear, "Oh, you gained some weight."

I am almost positive that this was the day that I began hating people. I just don't understand the point of telling me shit that I can obviously see for myself. I looked in the mirror that morning. I saw the same fucking acne that they did. I didn't notice the change in my weight though. When my clothes started getting too small, I thought that the fucking clothes fairy was sneaking into my closet and taking them in without my permission. I'm so thankful that they pointed out to me that I was just a gluttonous slob. I don't know what a 12-year-old would do without that advice.

I thought that I'd get over it once I survived puberty, but boy did becoming a young adult have a big fucking surprise in store for me! Once I began high school it was like all hell broke loose, and it burned through each and every filter on the mouths of those around me. No one seemed to care *what* they said to me, as long as it was said at the most inopportune moments. The backyard cookouts that I used to look forward to became the bane of my existence, and I swear my family started having more of them just to annoy me.

I didn't make the situation any better by being indecisive about my future. I take full responsibility for missing the memo that at 14 years old, I was supposed to have figured out what I wanted to do with my life in its entirety. How irresponsible of me! I should really have had that figured out specifically in order to fill out my school's five-year plan in a timely fashion. I admit it. I let everyone down. I didn't figure out my life in time to fill out a piece of paper. I don't even deserve the air that I breathe because I never thought of jotting down my plan to breathe it.

I don't remember what I ended up writing down on that Godforsaken piece of paper, but I do know that I made all of it up—*ALL* of it. There was not one fragment of that plan that actually appealed to me. I almost didn't use my real name, but that would have resulted in my guidance counselor pestering me to fill out another one, so I willingly scribbled my autograph onto my greatest work of fiction to date.

Perhaps this was karma working its magic, but somewhere between filling out that paper and becoming a high school junior, I won the lottery. Obviously I didn't win money because I couldn't legally buy a ticket. I did, however, hit the jackpot when it came to receiving more unwanted advice. The years prior to this were just practice. I could give pieces of it away to every human on the planet, and I'd still have far too much left over for myself.

It started when I *mentioned* going to college. I literally only *briefly* mentioned it once in the vicinity of some family and friends, but within an hour I was enrolled into six colleges with a list of eight majors that I needed to commit to. It didn't matter that I hadn't applied to these colleges, that I didn't *want* to apply to these colleges, *or* that I had zero interest in the subjects that I was being told to major in—this was the advice that I was awarded. It made me seriously wonder if any of these people even knew who the fuck I was. How could they, if they'd give me advice like that?

If that wasn't enough fun, there were the select few who were so antiestablishment that they suggested that I give two middle fingers to college all together. They'd been able to make it with just a high school education (or less), so why couldn't I? What made college so essential to *my* well being when high school was good enough for everyone else in the family? Oh, I don't know, maybe because in their time I could buy a house with like eight nickels, three cigarettes, five chickens, and a nice horse— just a thought.

It didn't stop there. The Military driven individuals had to make their case as to why the best path for me would be to enlist into the military, and live my life serving my country. This was probably some of the most respectable of advice, but the problem is that I'm about as athletic as a newborn giraffe—in fact, that's *exactly* what I look like when I'm running. I'd defeat any enemy in battle by making them laugh themselves into oblivion. I couldn't even get picked to play on a basketball team in my middle school gym class. Call me crazy, but I think the military may have required a tad more ability than what I had to offer, just a tad.

However, none of these pieces of unwanted advice was as unwanted as the comments discouraging my ideas. It didn't matter *what* I said, I was always told that there was something better that I could set my sights on. The hardest decision I've ever made was trying to figure out whether I was laughed at more when I said that I was thinking about becoming a yoga instructor, or when I said that I was considering becoming an English teacher.

I was supposed to be the smart one in the family! How in the world could I have possibly set my sights so low? Besides, a person with social anxiety would never be able to pull off either of those careers. What the hell was I thinking? It wasn't like there were treatment options available to assist with leading a "normal" life or anything.

I mean, instilling knowledge into willing participants is sweet, and helping people to simultaneously establish a mind-body connection while getting into shape is noble, but those careers don't pay enough money. What I *really* needed to do was get super educated and become a doctor or a lawyer. It didn't matter that I'd spend most of my life in debt from the student loans, or that I had no desire to do any of those jobs. That's what I needed to do with the *one* life that I'd been given. I needed to spend it doing something that I hated— 'cuz money!

I barely made it through the monotony of high school with my sanity. I was mentally unable to partake in one more endeavor that I didn't want to do. My philosophy is that life is all about crossing off the items on my bucket list. I *need* the thrill of doing things that excite me in order to enjoy my life, which brings me back to my initial thought of wondering if any of these people knew who the fuck I was. Then I realized that they didn't know, and what's more is that they couldn't have, because *I* didn't know who I was. I still don't know.

The problem is that no one can tell me who I am. No one can tell anyone who they are. We are born with the burden of trying to figure it out, and we exist with the burden of trying to figure it out on a strict timeline that we created as a society. When shit starts going badly we begin to blame our unhappiness on society, but we ARE society. We can't change it unless we change ourselves (and ignore several people in the process).

I don't know who I am, and that's why you don't know who I am either. There's no way for me to tell you, because I don't know. I'm working on it though, and if it gives you any comfort, I'm trying much harder than I did on that five year plan.

-X

Dreams

Imagine this: During the entire course of your life there has been *one* gift that you've always wanted on Christmas morning (or whatever it is that you celebrate that allows you to receive a gift), and you were always told that it would come at later time. Then one Christmas, as you pluck your gift from beneath the tree, your family informs you that this will be the last one that you'll ever receive for the rest of your life. Would you still be excited to open the gift, or would you be filled with anxiety? I think any sane person would experience a significant amount of panic.

That's what becoming a young adult feels like to me. It seems like the last chance to claim success, or it'll be lost forever. I'll be forced to live a life of mediocrity, and I'll die with the burden of failure on my mind. To be honest with you, I don't know why it feels that way, but I know it's the scariest fucking thing that's ever been thrown my way.

The only feeling worse than that is when you wake up and realize that the dream that you thought you wanted may not be the one that you *actually* want. Conveniently, this usually occurs after you've already invested lots of time and even more money into becoming whatever that dream is. The dread that comes with having a *ridiculously* expensive piece of paper (like a degree or license) that you don't even want to use is like buying a car and finding out that gas is no longer in existence. The realization that you don't know what to do next, but that you need to do something quickly, is the most gut wrenching experience known to sanity. This is known as a quarter life crisis, but that's a different story for a different breakdown.

Our career goals are painted as the highlight of our lives. When people ask who you are, the next question tends to be, "What do you do for a living?" It has become the way that our human value is assessed. It's like we were given a mansion, but we try to determine how much it is worth based solely on the condition of the guest bathroom. We don't look at the bigger picture when we need to, and that's why things are not working for us.

Until this point, we've spent our entire lives trying to become *something* when we didn't know who we were to begin with. We literally picked a random thing and decided to dedicate our entire young life working toward becoming whatever it is. By the time we realize that we may have made a mistake, we feel backed into a corner by the need to make money, and we settle for a career that we hate. It happens all the time.

There's another side to this though. I used to think that the people who knew (or thought that they knew) early in childhood what they wanted to become as adults were the luckiest people alive. They didn't have to stress about what to do as a junior in high school, because they already knew what they were going to do. The only thing that they had to worry about was actually doing it. Then one day I met up with an old classmate who used to want nothing more than to be a doctor. It isn't my place to tell this kid's story, so let's just say that due to circumstances beyond her control she will never be able to become a doctor. She switched career choices, and now she's sitting right beside me in the boat that's stuck up shit creek.

There is a very good chance that I'm desperately trying to make myself feel better by looking at things this way, but it made me very happy that I never knew what I wanted to be as a kid. If I had picked something and it didn't work out, then I would have had to sand down and paint over a picture that I'd created and coveted since childhood. If I had to end up in this boat anyway, then I'm thankful that I got here without dropping my dream into the creek of shit while trying to get into the boat, losing the paddle was enough.

She isn't my only former classmate in this position either. I actually know more people whose childhood dreams have failed than I know whose dreams have worked out. The immediate reflex of others is to blame that person for their dream not working out, but I think that's a coping mechanism. It's as though we're incapable of admitting that sometimes things just don't work out. I understand the need to not be pessimistic, but we need to be realistic.

No one grows up with the intention of wanting to be a delivery guy (or gal); we tend to pick very "glamorous" dreams. However, there are a lot of people who are doing those jobs, and I'm pretty sure that they didn't plan it that way. That's just the way that life worked out. Furthermore, we NEED people to do those jobs—those totally respectable, very real jobs that deserve the *same* appreciation that the "fancy" jobs get.

However, when we are impressionable, small children, no one tells us that our dreams may not come true. It is practically taboo to tell a kid that shit happens, or that it may be slightly impossible to become the thing that you want to be if that thing is a horse. I don't know why the genius who assumed that this ignorance would be blissful thought that this was a good idea, but that person didn't think this shit through. We spend, like, the first five years that we can actually remember thinking that we can become anything in the world—literally, *anything* in the world.

When I was in kindergarten, we had to draw a picture of what we wanted to be when we grew up. If this had been assigned a mere two years prior, then I'm certain that my ass would have been at the table scribbling my best impression of Rover, which was the name of the dog that I wanted to be. My other early aspiration of wanting to be a cashier for the sole purpose of being able to operate the "catching wheel" (cash register) had become slightly less glamorous to me as well, so I didn't know what I wanted to do with my life. (Yes, I was actually confused this early in life. I realize now that I didn't stand a chance at having it together by high school.) Being the little perfectionist that I am, I could *not* leave my paper blank…so I drew my teacher.

Yes, I may have been an indecisive ass kisser, but the kid next to me drew a fucking fire truck. No, not a fireman, he wanted to be *the truck*. At least I knew that I had to be a human; I did have that going for me.Our teacher had no choice except to "ooh" and "ahh" at his aspirations. I'm more than sure that if she hadn't, Little Chevrolet's parents would have wanted to run her over for destroying their kid's dream. Therefore, we have to find out the hard way—all on our own—that some dreams can only happen while we're asleep.

I, for one, think that's bullshit. That's like telling someone all the benefits and joy of a home fireplace, but not telling that person that the exact same fireplace can set the entire house on fire if the chimney is not properly maintained. It may not be a lie, but it is an omission of the truth and that's not any better because it can still hurt someone.

Furthermore, asking kids what they want to be when they grow up, and expecting them to pick one thing is insinuating that we can only have one dream for our lives. Why is it that we feel so limited? We aren't married to our dreams or anything; no one gets hurt if we have more than one. It isn't cheating. If one doesn't work out, then we know that we have the option of chasing another one. Isn't that much more realistic than to pretend that we're guaranteed to land our first dream job, and that we only need to have one dream?

The world isn't outlined in black and white, but we often pretend that it is. Society will tell us that we can be anything, but then turn around and criticize people who don't have "real" jobs. What if that was the thing that they picked? No one seemed to mind when these kids wanted to be dogs and fire trucks. Is being a pizza delivery person really worse than that?

So, yeah, I used to feel pretty bummed about the fact that I never really had a childhood dream of "being" anything, but now I'm pretty glad that things happened that way. I didn't grow up with one vision in mind only to be extremely disappointed later. I am one of the lucky ones.

Some of us have to find our dreams, and that's no easy feat. It can take years before you stumble upon the thing that'll make you happier than all the other things that you could have been. One day, on no one else's timeline, you'll find a thing that fits perfectly with who you are—even if it isn't high paying or glamorous. It won't be until your dreams start keeping you awake that you'll realize that you've finally found it. When you do, you have to at least attempt to go after it. If you don't, the regrets will very easily turn your dreams into a nightmare.

-X

Quarter Life Crisis

I have been late accomplishing just about every milestone that I have reached in life. I started walking at a late age, and heaven knows I never learned to crawl forward. I was weaned at a very late age as well, and by very late, I mean that I was already in grade school. Though I'm not one to embrace confrontation, it can be argued that I'm still waiting for that glorious moment when puberty hits me like a bus and I get my adult body.

You get the point; I take late blooming to a new level. There is only one thing that I have been early for, and that is a quarter life crisis. In fact, I think I'm having my third one and I'm still not at the age that we consider a quarter of a life—that practically makes me an expert on this stuff.

I wish I could give you a formal definition of a quarter life crisis, but I looked it up, and the consensus was something along the lines of: "Feelings of anxiety about the direction of one's life." Saying that this definition is an understatement is a **wildly offensive** understatement.

Do you know the feeling that you get when you wake up and realize that your alarm clock didn't go off? Well, for me, it's a horrifying moment when my heart becomes an anchor that sinks into the trenches of my pinky toe, *just* as my stomach feels like it's about to somersault right out of my ass. The sweat starts pouring like water, and I frantically start trying to get my shit together to do as much damage control as I possibly can to my schedule.

The problem is that I'm in such a rush that I start messing up everything, even the simple things that used to be second nature to me. I start dropping things because I'm trying to move so quickly, and I just end up making a bigger and *bigger* mess until I finally feel like I've screwed up to the point of no possible return. I lose all hope of ever making it to my destination on time, and I decide to just crawl back into bed. My definition of a quarter life crisis is when I wake up and feel like *that* every single second that I'm awake.

As the weeks roll away, returning to bed becomes futile because life itself is now a perpetual nightmare in which despite knowing that I absolutely *must* be somewhere, I can't figure out where the hell I'm supposed to be going. The only thing that I know with absolute certainty is that I'm late, *again*. I don't know what I'm late for, and I can't find the keys to my car anyway. Whether the alarm goes off in the morning or not, I'm always late beyond repair. Always.

My existence has become a tug of war between relentless anxiety and soul crushing depression. I know that it doesn't seem like those two emotions belong together since depression seems like moping, and anxiety is usually panic and urgency, but they have found a way to work together. You see, first, I'll feel anxious about trying to accomplish everything on the long list of things that my "know-it-all" childhood self set out for me to accomplish.

When I discover that it is almost impossible to do all of those things (because my world view was so skewered when I made this God-awful thing), then I become depressed because there's no way to remedy the failure. The time is already gone. Hope slips through my fingers like Siesta Beach's sand, and I sink into bed until it hits me again that *all of that fucking time is GONE*. It's *never* coming back, and it's *still* passing. The next thing I know, I'm right back to acting as though I washed down a helping of Speed with a large cup of coffee and a few energy drinks, desperately trying to accomplish 56 life goals in about a week's time.

Those emotions are unpleasant, but the worst part of a quarter life crisis are the "experts" (or older members of society) who firmly believe that I am making all of this shit up for attention. There are actually people in this world who believe that they know *so* much about a stranger that they can tell me *how* I'm feeling, *what* I'm feeling, and *why* I'm feeling it. Most importantly, they can tell *me* all of this MUCH better than I can tell *them*. I know I'm confused about my life, but this is ridiculously bold of them.

If you're anything like these "experts," then you probably think that I'm exaggerating and that I need to pay close attention to the things that these people are telling me. Obviously they survived the same crisis that I'm struggling with, so they should have the answers that I'm searching for. That may be true to an extent, but the world that they were living in is vastly different from the world we're living in now. Their rules don't always apply anymore.

Besides, it's not like these experts were ever *me* going through *my* quarter life crisis. They may be able to give me general guidelines about how to cope with my feelings, but I'm the only one with the backstage pass to an exclusive viewing of all the behind-the-scenes breakdowns. I'm an individual, and though I feel like I know absolutely nothing about my life, I **do** know when a solution isn't working for me. In fact, all I know is what *isn't* right with my life. That's why I'm having a damn crisis.

Things haven't improved since the last dreadful morning that I woke up in unexplainable panic. In fact, they got a little worse when morning after morning I found myself waking up in the same house that I grew up in—meaning I realized that I still lived with my parents. I'm sure that my parents mean well, and they are some of the most lovely humans that I've met, but I don't know if they understand how much not having my own place makes me feel like I'm faking adulthood.

It isn't their fault that we've been ingrained to believe that moving out is THE ultimate sign of growing up, but the fact remains that other people in society will most likely look down on just about anyone who is still living at home past high school graduation.

The logical side of me knows that unless I start completely wasting my life by not even trying to find my way, or my parents want me to move out, then my job should be to completely ignore those people. I'll go so far as to say that as long as my parents and I have a working agreement with this situation, I shouldn't worry about moving out at *all*. I know that I'm not less of an adult because I sleep in the same home with my parents, because there are cultures in which *many* generations live together, but I don't *feel* that way. I feel like a bird sitting in its nest while everyone awaits the moment when I take flight, but no one has noticed that I only have one wing.

It's quite possible that you're reading this because you're having a quarter life crisis as well, so I just want to warn you that the worst part of a crisis like this is the judgment that you'll receive from others. It is the one time in life when you need all the love and support that you can handle, but you're often criticized, called spoiled or lazy, and blamed for feeling the way that you feel.

The mental chaos of a quarter life crisis is not to be underestimated. It starts off innocently enough with asking yourself, "What do I want to do with my life?" However, soon that question turns into, "Why can't I figure out what I want to do with my life? What's wrong with me? Why can't I figure this out? I should be able to figure this out! I'm too old to still be making this decision. I should have known the answer to this when I was four. I mean, that's the proper order to learn things, right? Learn to sit up, learn to crawl, learn to walk, learn to talk, learn to spell my name, and then figure out the rest of my life in its entirety."

The next thing you know, you're spiraling down an emotional tunnel, and you don't even know where it leads to because there is no possible way that you can go any further down than you already are unless you completely fall off the planet. Suddenly, everything seems like it is too much to handle. Creating a budget, running errands, hanging out with friends or family, all of it is just too much. This is the equivalent of the moment when you decide to go back to bed on the morning that you're late. You've accidentally created a mess that is too big for you to clean up all at once, so you'll just go back to bed until you develop a course of action.

Your main problem is probably that you're either unemployed, *or* you're working a low paying, dead-end job. First of all, if you're working a shitty job, you don't get to complain as much as those who are unemployed. It isn't ideal, but at least you're generating *some* income. You can feel some sense of independence when you're able to pay for your own cell phone, gas, or grocery bill. You're actually not as behind as you think you are, which is great. Sure, you may throw up a little bit in your mouth when it's time to clock in, but you don't have to stay here forever. You're allowed to do more than one thing as an adult, remember?

If you're unemployed, then the most important thing that you can do for yourself is never stop looking for a job. If you can find an odd job, it'll feel a *lot* better than anything should. In the meantime, the only advice that I can offer you is what I'm doing now: give thanks that your family loves you enough to make sure that you aren't homeless.

Seriously, being unemployed sucks. It is probably the factor that hits the hardest, because we live in a society that has come to equate who we are with what we do to make money. That is not the case. There is more to us than what we do for a living, but it will not feel like that in the throes of a crisis. In fact, it'll feel like your self-worth is directly related to how much you make, and if you're not making anything, then you can understand the problem here. The only remedy is to find a job or hobby. You cannot force anyone to hire you. The only thing that you can do is keep applying at various places. While that isn't working, try to do something that you've always wanted to do, like, oh I don't know, start a blog. :)

The misery of a quarter life crisis can increase tenfold if you are single. This is another one of the more difficult aspects to deal with because you cannot plan romantic fulfillment, most of the time it comes unexpectedly. Your parents can't fix that. The best thing your friends or family can do is fix you up on dates— which you may or may not regret within two minutes of meeting this person. Loneliness rules during this prime time slot. Every time you're preparing to go to sleep (or wake up) you'll be sure to remember how alone you are, because you'll look to the other side of the bed and realize that no one else is there. You'll forget the fact that until this point in your life, **most** of the time no one was *ever* there. All of a sudden, another person is required for you to appreciate the fact that you have a bed to sleep in. That's bullshit.

Since quarter life crises are thrifty little bitches, your loneliness will join forces with your knowledge of basic biology (especially if you're female, but males aren't immune) and bring you to your knees in tears about the fact that you'll never have those kids that you don't even want. You know for a fact that your biological clock will have ticked its last tock long before anyone would ever decide to spend their life with you. I mean, have you taken a look at yourself lately? You have absolutely *nothing* going for you. You can't remember the last time you went on a date or found someone who was interested in you. In fact, you're pretty sure that your sexual attractiveness feature is broken. You wouldn't even date yourself, because obviously you aren't going anywhere in life.

Still, loneliness isn't the problem so much as the fact that being single at this time has serious potential to make you feel left out. Everyone and their grandmother's balding donkey is getting engaged, married, or having kids, and you're just here laying in bed watching the seventh season of some "reality" show while eating an entire bag of chips, and half a box of cookies. You'll start getting invited to weddings and baby showers for your best friends, and you won't even feel happy about it.

The first time that you don't feel happy for a friend or family member may scare you. In fact, it'll probably set off a slew of other emotions that are common in these situations, the first of which is guilt. Yes, the guilt will punch you directly in the esophagus and leave you unable to speak. You won't even be able to properly congratulate your friend, but on the bright side, you won't say anything stupid about why this big event isn't even that great either. How many people have done what they're about to do anyway? You know what a lot of people haven't accomplished? Finishing a Legend of Zelda video game in a week or less. THAT is a fucking feat! All of this marriage and childbirth shit is just a trap. You know better, and *you* aren't falling for it like those idiots!

After the guilt has eaten its allotted portion of your soul, the self doubt and insecurity will set your living remains on fire. These two feelings can be so strong that you may start to think that they're teaming up to try to kill you, and maybe they are. See, insecurity will make you feel like you don't know if you're making the right choices. Then the self-doubt shows up and convinces you that there is no *way* that you have the ability to make the right choice, even if it was the only choice that you had.

I mean, after all, you're YOU. You haven't accomplished what you hoped to, so obviously you're completely incapable of ever doing any other thing properly. Your life will forever be a fucking travesty. When you start having *those* thoughts, when you know for a fact that something that *you haven't even done yet* is a failure, then you can be sure of one thing and one thing only—you are eyelash deep in a quarter life crisis.

It's a vicious cycle that doesn't seem to have an end because you're pushing to do something that is impossible to do. You're trying to accomplish something that you set your sights on at a time when you had to ask permission to use the bathroom. That's why your next step is to take that list and burn the ever-loving piss out of it. That won't accomplish anything, but it'll make you feel better. Your dreams going up in smoke is not a bad thing when they were the reason you were miserable.

The next, and admittedly more productive, thing that you'll do is to make a new plan—don't you DARE make it five years long. I swear to you, that's a creation of the school system that's designed to destroy your spirit. There's no way that you can see into the future to know what your circumstances will be in five years, and lets be honest, that would just stress you out even more. What you *can* do is figure out what is best right now, and how to get to the next best thing once you've accomplished the immediate goals.

If you need a job, start job hunting for something that will cover as many of your expenses as possible. If you want to go back to school, apply and see if there are any scholarships or grants available for you. If you're lonely, try to go on dates or hang out with friends. If you're feeling confused about your spiritual beliefs, then get out and study different ones. What I'm saying is that, in my opinion, the best remedy for a quarter life crisis is to cut off its oxygen source—which is trying to plan your entire life to the letter.

Life is not a liner function. It is a scatter plot with absolutely no guarantee of a visible pattern. If you plan too far ahead into the future, then you're bound to fail at some point. (I don't recommend never planning either, but you shouldn't have lunch dates scheduled for two years into the future.) I could get all hippie love child on you, and explain why you need to be able to flux and flow in life. However, I won't do that to you. You're already confused, so I'll keep it simple by saying something that is almost too cliché for me to type: take one day at a time, brace yourself for anything while expecting nothing, and don't quit breathing.

-X

Childhood Sucks

One thing that I have noticed since becoming a young adult is that I frequently overhear my peers wishing that they were kids again. Perhaps it's because I was bullied as a kid, but I do not share this sentiment. As confusing as life is right now, I'd rather come *through* the confusion than to go back to a time when I didn't even know that such relentless chaos existed.

I think the real problem at hand is that often times we look to the past with a *thick* pair of rose colored glasses on, amplifying the positive aspects, and completely overlooking the negative aspects. When we are kids, the only topics we talk about are the awesome things that we'll do when we grow up. We can't wait to be more like our parents—but cooler. We start backing down from that statement before we even graduate from high school. In other words, while caught up in the confusion of adulthood, we have forgotten why we thought childhood sucked in the first place. Let me offer this post as a gentle smack in the face to jog everyone's memory.

First of all, you cannot make any decisions for yourself when you're a child. I know what you're thinking right now, "I still can't make any decisions for myself." Well, no, you *can*. You're just afraid to make the wrong one. That's totally different. You have a right to make your own decisions now. Do you want to eat the broccoli? No? Then you don't have to eat it! You don't want to clean your room? You don't have to clean it! Do you want ice cream for breakfast? No one is stopping you. You don't feel like going to bed at this moment? Stay awake until you pass out. The decision is yours. You're allowed to make your own choices. This is not the case with childhood.

Next, you weren't allowed to drive. Do you remember what life was like before you had your permit or driver's license? If you're wishing to be a kid again, then I don't think you remember because it *sucked*. You had to ask your parents to bring you everywhere, and if they didn't feel like being your personal chauffeur, then you had to stay home. Seriously, don't you remember how mind numbingly angry that made you? Car notes, car insurance, and gas are expensive, but being able to go where you want to go, whenever you want to go there, is priceless. It is a rare gem that we are not legally allowed to have in childhood.

When you become an adult, you have the opportunity to make your own money. I mean, unless you're a child actor or something of that nature, you cannot hold a regular job until you're about 15 or 16, depending on your state of residence. The only thing that sucked more than not being able to drive was not being able to buy anything that you wanted. Sure, you may think that your parents bought you everything, but I'm sure there was at least one occasion when you wanted to disown them in the grocery store because they wouldn't buy you a boxed, food-like substance that you didn't need anyway. You may still be broke, but at least you have the opportunity to make money. You don't have to wait for Grandma and Grandpa to come over and slip money into your hand when your parents aren't looking. You have hope now.

How could we forget everyone's favorite? School! You were literally forced to go to school until you were 16 years old. If you didn't go, then your parents could be arrested and put in jail (which makes me question whether or not parents actually own their kids, but that's another thought for another time). Anyway, school had to be the worst part of childhood, and no one seems to remember this. First of all, you had to wake up at approximately dicks o'clock in the morning to be there. My school started at 7:15 a.m. *sharp*. That means as a kid, I had a 5:30 a.m. wake up time. That could not have been healthy.

If that wasn't enough, you were expected to *actually* be able to learn and function even though you probably stayed up late doing homework and studying. That had to be the worst part about school—it followed you home. You spent seven to seven and a half hours a day at the school, then you had to go home and spend another three to four hours on homework and studying. That is at least ten hours a day. That is 50 hours a week, minimum! Where is our overtime?

That doesn't even take into account the students who were in the extracurricular activities that we were encouraged to join, nor commute time, or the time spent studying for things like the ACT, SAT, and GEE. With all of this taken into account, we were still expected to make straight A's, have a social life, do our chores, spend time with the family, and sleep eight hours a night—when studies suggest that we needed ten hours of sleep anyway. That shit was inhumane, and I am overjoyed that those days are behind me, even though I'm spending most of the time that I gained confused.

The point that I'm trying to make is that, sure, adulthood is hard, but so was childhood. Life in general is hard, but that doesn't mean that it has to be completely awful. I think a lot of the misery of adulthood is brought upon us by ourselves. We are still trying to measure our success on a grading scale, restricting ourselves to be nothing more than numbers and averages. If that lifestyle made us miserable in the past, then it'll make us miserable now. We convince ourselves that we need a certain type of car, a certain size house, a visit to "x" number of countries on our list of experience, and a large sum of money in the bank. That is not success. Success is having what we need and still being happy while we have it.

I like nice cars just as much as the next person, but if I have to work 80 hours a week, pay more for insurance than I do for my healthcare, and worry about getting a minor scratch on it every time it leaves the garage, then I've failed. How? Well, for starters I grew up to be owned by a car and it's not even a kick-ass Autobot like in Transformers. That's fucked up! Secondly, if I spend more time worrying about keeping a thing in pristine condition instead of enjoying it, then I've done something wrong. Finally, if I spend so much time working to keep a luxury that I don't even have enough *time* to enjoy it, then it's no longer a luxury. I've purchased a very expensive depressant.

I don't know how you all are doing this adult thing, but I do know that overthinking can make it a miserable experience. The good news is that you have the freedom to do what you want to do. If you have the luxury of knowing (and controlling) what is making you sad, then just stop doing the thing that makes you sad. You're an adult now; you can do that. It won't be easy, but there is a possibility in adulthood where there was not one in childhood. That's why you wanted to be an adult in the first place, remember?

Besides, the vital parts of your childhood may survive into adulthood if you play your cards right. You are allowed to keep your imagination. You are allowed to play video games with all of your free time. You can watch whatever you want, no matter how "dirty" it is. You can stay out as late as you want to. (Well, you can if you didn't get married.) You can make your own money. You can always have your friends over at your place. You can drive. There doesn't have to be any more school if you don't want there to be. You can eat those terrible, sugary foods for breakfast. And if you're *really* lucky, your grandparents will still slip you a $20 bill into your hand when your parents aren't looking, because no matter how much you grow up, you'll always be their grandchild.

-X

The Gap

Did you know that when you're an infant, there is a little chart at the doctor's office that tells your parents approximately what age you should be when you accomplish certain milestones, such as rolling over, sitting up, and things of that nature? The majority of infants reach their milestones at the age that this chart says that they should. Those who do not reach their milestones "on time" drive their parents absolutely crazy, because they fear that something is wrong with their child. Generally, I hit most of my milestones, but as I've mentioned before, I never learned to crawl forward. (That's right, I crawled backwards.) In addition to that, it took me forever and a day to learn how to walk. Sometimes, I'm still not quite sure that I've mastered it.

If you walk into your doctor's office as an adult, you'll (hopefully) find that there is no longer a chart that tells you when you should reach certain milestones in your life. I blame this entirely on the existence of young adults, because at this age, there is no telling what we're doing. There are some people who are homeowners and married with kids at age 23, but then there are others at age 23 who are too drunk to find their parents' home, let alone own one of their own. There is an infinite number of degrees of "adultness" between these two extremes. I like to call this giant difference "The Gap." (No, not like the store with the overpriced clothes.)

This gap causes a ton of anxiety for young adults and parents alike. I can only imagine what would happen if there was a chart that tried to predict when we should complete college, have an AWESOME career, travel the world, get married, buy a house, and maybe have a kid. Most people try to fit all of that into ten years, you know, before they turn 30 and die. We experience quarter life crises at an alarming rate as it is, not to mention the suicide rate is increasing for young adults. If there were such a chart, then I think we'd all be assigned a psychiatrist upon reaching age sixteen, just like we all had pediatricians in childhood. I mean, there *is* a suggested, unspoken timeline that we all seem to be aware of, but not following it doesn't insinuate that something is developmentally wrong with us…it just *really* feels like there is.

Among my peers, we seem to be divided right down the center of the two extremes. What I find so amazing is that when I overhear their conversations, each side tries to make it sound as though they are having the *best* time of their lives. I listen as the "adult" group talk about how great it is to have kids, and be settled down, and how it's *totally* okay that they didn't get to have the college experience or travel. They have their kids (and sometimes a spouse), and that's all they'll ever need in life. Not to mention, they are in *love* with their jobs. They get to sit at a desk, crunch numbers, and be constantly observed by their bosses. They also get to do grown up things, like get drug tested, do taxes, hide the same tattoos that they disobeyed their parents to get from their bosses, and have a closet full of "office appropriate" clothing. The only regret they have is that it didn't happen sooner. Life is so incredibly perfect!

I have an extremely hard time believing that.

On the other hand, the "adulthood challenged" group, which I think I may be the awkward stepchild of, doesn't lie any better. I often hear how they are so glad that they are single. They never want to leave college, and they never want to be tied down. Family? Why have that when they can spend the night on a dance floor with other sweaty, drunk people? They have the pleasure, honor, and privilege of helping their drunken friend puke into a respectable area.

Why would they own a home or apartment? That's just a ball and chain to their future plans of backpacking across Europe! They'll *totally* do that once they have some emergency money saved, and they'll start saving that as soon as they find a job. It'll be a temporary one, of course. They're too young to be faced with the possibility of having to be stuck at one job for the rest of their lives. To hell with a little security! Bring on that Goddamned uncertainty!

Seriously, do either of those groups sound appealing to you? One glance at the adult group, and I want to just skip to part where I become a crazy old person in the nursing home. However, a glance at the adulthood challenged group makes me question my faith in humanity. As I've said before, I'm closer to the adult challenged group, but I don't fit in there either. I'm caught somewhere between these two extremes.

I can openly admit that I'd like (some) stability. I'd love to be married someday. I want the problem of taxes, because it means I'd be making money. However, I've only been to a nightclub one time before I decided that it was not for me. I don't do drugs. I don't smoke. I don't even consume soda, let alone alcohol. I grab a juice box when I'm feeling really hot and dangerous.

As for dating, I never really thought about it seriously before the past couple of years. You can use that bit of information to fill in the rest of the blanks yourself about what other "young adult milestones" I haven't reached. I don't even know if that makes me more mature or less mature than the people who are accidentally reaching these particular milestones due to the effects of alcohol.

I think the real problem with being a young adult today is that we've been provided with a stock image of what adulthood is supposed to look like, but one size *never* fits all. A lot of us cannot get there while others have gotten there too quickly (though some in both groups did look genuinely happy, just not most of them). If this is the case, then I guess I'm okay with being in the "what the hell are you even doing with your life?" group, because while I do feel anxiety about it, it also means that I still have a blank slate. I'd rather face criticism for starting my painting "too late" than to rush into it, and paint the wrong picture.

So yes, if there was a chart of milestones for young adults to reach, then I'm 1000% sure that I would miss 95% of them. I still live with my parents. I have never had a significant other. I've never been on a date. First kiss? Oh please, I'm too busy playing video games for that! Saturday morning, with all of its glorious animation, is still the best time in the world to me. Also, if the mood should hit me, I *will* spend hours of my time alone with a good coloring book. These are innocent, simple pleasures that make me *ridiculously* happy. It doesn't make any sense to me that these little things should determine whether or not I'm "grown up" enough for society.

If young adulthood is about being reckless, then I guess I'm not truly a young adult. If adulthood is about denying myself harmless pleasures to prove that I can be a society's generic interpretation of an adult, then I guess I'll just never really be an adult in their eyes. Clearly I'm okay with skipping milestones. I wasn't afraid to tell you that never learned to crawl, and maybe that's a sign that I'm finally starting to walk in this whole adulthood journey. I'll get there when I get there. Regardless of how I did it, I've always made it—eventually.

-X

The Holidays as a Young Adult

As I've mentioned before, when I was a kid I never thought that there would come a time in my life when I would absolutely *loathe* family events, but I *never* thought that I'd dislike Christmas. I used to be filled with a special excitement when the holiday season was near—you know, like some time in October. I'd begin a countdown of anticipation leading up to the cold, overcast days filled with hearty food, extended family, sparkly decorations, and occasionally, gifts.

I would be so insanely excited about the Christmas holidays that I didn't question the weird events that were taking place around me, such as why it was okay for a strange man to secretly watch me all year, or why the hell there was a six foot tree in the middle of my living room. I just went along with it, because I was getting ridiculously expensive presents. However, I became a young adult, and all of that changed without my permission.

There is this thing that happens as we get older, and it's that we're expected to do stuff—hard stuff. That alone isn't the problem. The problem is that our families may think that it is time for us to do those things before we're ready to do them, and there seems to be no rule about what can be said to us to convey their displeasure when our performance does not meet their expectations. The first time that this happened to me, I was caught so off guard by their words that I could only stare at them blankly, questioning with every fabric of my being why the hell they would say something so hurtful to me at a time like this.

My intentions for the holiday celebrations were to tease my cousins, open gifts to find items that I'd wanted all year, laugh at my drunken relatives, and eat until I drifted off into the second stages of a food coma. Instead, I was faced with many hostile, insensitive questions that left me feeling like the world's biggest underachiever. I saw some of these people only once a year, and when I did, I was disappointing them. I now realize that this is a common experience for young adults, so I thought I should give you a warning as to what the holidays are like for us now.

It is usually subtle in the beginning. You'll greet your loved one, and he or she will tell you how much you've grown. The first step of a holiday event is affirming that you are indeed a legitimate human being who grows as you age. That is the first prerequisite, and you have it! As a reward, you get to graduate to the phase where you'll be questioned about your love life. It may even come attached to a compliment. It'll sound something like, "Oh wow! You've grown up to be so good looking! Who is the lucky guy or girl?" Don't be fooled. While I'm sure you're a great looking person, the prying question is the true intention here. The wonderful compliment just serves as a distraction to prevent you from becoming too defensive. (I also don't understand why the need to reinforce the idea that beauty equals love is always on your family's agenda, but that's a different matter.)

If you're in a relationship, then be prepared to answer a 250 question exam about your significant other. I cannot provide you with a complete study guide, because there are some variations in exam format. However, the basic topics will include: past and present employment, education, past and present place of residence, past relationships, physical appearance, and future goals and plans.

If you are not in a relationship, then you should prepare for your exam by studying a series of extremely simple questions. Once informed of your current relationship status, your family will become worried about you and begin to ask you simple questions such as: your current age, the last time you went on a date, the last time you went out on the town, and how you plan to remedy your singleness. Once the exam is complete, it is imperative that you gently remind your family that being single is *not* an illness. There is no need to remedy the absence of a romantic relationship, because it is not vital to a happy, successful life. You can try to gently tell them this by explaining that you'd rather be single than to be in a relationship with the wrong person.

If you're unemployed, then you have my sympathy, because your family is about to give you the hardest exam of your young adult life. It is given in essay format, and the sole question is, "Well, what are you planning on doing with your life?" Your answer here is crucial. If you're planning to enter into any type of educational institution, then you may be safe, as long as your field of concentration is appeasing to this particular family member. The good news is that you don't have to wait for the results. You will know immediately how your plan faired judging by the look on your loved one's face, as well as the amount of advice you are given afterward.

If you receive a passing grade, then your family will reply, "That's awesome. I'm so proud of you." However, if you fail the exam, then your family will reply with an answer that begins with, "What you should do is…" If you have a harsher family, then the reply may be, "That's stupid. You're wasting your time. You need to do something else."

After the initial disapproval of your plan, you'll be asked why you chose that option at all. Despite the answer that you give, you'll be told why your reasoning is completely invalid. The loved one will begin to lecture you with a slew of information about job markets, the cost of living, and other statistics. This is your remediation class. It is designed for those who have forgotten how to live their lives. Luckily, before you are born your family takes a class on your life. That way, if you ever forget how to live it properly, they'll be able to correct you.

You will not be off the hook solely due to employment. First of all, regardless of your prior experience, you must be working at what is considered a "real job" in order to pass the exam. This means that the majority of jobs in most retail establishments, major fast food chains, or freelance positions are considered invalid. Occasionally, there are exceptions for individuals who hold management positions, but that is left to the discretion of the examiner. If your job passes its authentication test, then the pay must exceed approximately $35,000 per year regardless of your age, or place of residence. Positions of employment that fall below this minimum are considered to be below your potential, especially if you completed college (like everyone else).

Family is a weird entity. They are the people who are required by unwritten law to love you more than any of the other people on the planet do. However, they are simultaneously the people who have the power to make you more miserable than any of the other people on the planet can, and sometimes they take advantage of that power. Your job is to remember that despite what your family says, you cannot do anything about a problem until *you're* ready to make a change. Well, I mean you can act to please your family, but the result will probably end up being something totally opposite from what you wanted for yourself.

If you want to stay sane, then you have to remember that *most* of the time, your family is questioning you about these things because they want the best for you. If you're in the other position where your family is genuinely verbally abusive to you, then I have some great news for you. You're an adult now, and you don't have to talk to them if you do not wish to do so. If someone is causing you to experience every negative emotion known to man just by being in your presence, then it is time to question which one of you have the problem. Yes, there is the possibility that something is wrong with you, but there is also the possibility that this person is just an asshole. There are *tons* of people who are assholes, so be sure to carefully consider the possibility of this option.

However, you might just be in a bad place in your life. If you're half-assing everything, portraying your best role as a sitting duck, partying your life away, not taking care of your health, and generally being irresponsible, then your family would be wrong not to hold you accountable. That's what you do when you care about someone, you hold them accountable for their actions, because those actions may severely hurt them one day.

For example, if you are complaining about not having enough money for your bills, yet you're finding money to get drunk every weekend, then it may be time to think about who has the problem in this situation. If you are not actively trying to remedy your hardships, then you have no right to complain about them. Your unwillingness to deal with a situation does not make the situation go away, but it does make it a bigger problem once you're *forced* to deal with it.

I get it. Your family is annoying. Everyone's family is annoying at some point. They ask questions about your biggest insecurities, and the thought of being faced with that type of interrogation could send the calmest of people into a panic. However, most of the advice is formed with good intentions. If you're at a place in your life where you cannot accept advice (or constructive criticism) from people who truly have your best interests at heart, then perhaps you *are* the problem.

That's okay though. There are times in your life when you're almost supposed to be the problem, and growing up is one of those times. You're confused. You're lost. You're scared, and life makes you feel like you could vomit your soul at any given moment. You're allowed to be imperfect, just own up to your imperfections and eat some of that holiday food when things are getting rough. The holiday season is a short portion of your life, and you can handle unpleasant things short term. That's how you become an adult, or at least an adult like creature who can survive the holiday season.

-X

Lies

"Too old" is a lie we often tell,
When inside of anxiety's walls we dwell.
Society offers media as proof,
To convince the young they have no youth.
Racing thoughts and mental blocks,
Jam the doors that are still unlocked.
Retired to ageism's cluttered shelves,
We steal the greatness from ourselves.

Getting Older

There is a very specific part of growing up that seems to freak everyone out, and that's the part where we get older. The actual event of the number of years we've been on the Earth growing larger is not the problem. It's the expectations that are attached to that larger number that scare us. It's an undeniable fact of life. We're going to grow older, society will expect it to completely change who we are, our worth will be based on it, and there isn't a damn thing any of us can do to stop it. Still, I feel as though I'm one of the few people left out there who doesn't think that getting older has to be a completely horrendous experience. (That's probably another reason people think that I'm crazy.)

Perhaps I was subconsciously conditioned to believe that getting older isn't the end of excitement and happiness because I started going grey at the ripe old age of ten. The doctors initially blamed it on the stress of my social anxiety, but I know that it is no coincidence that my Grandfather's hair was at least 20% grey by the age of 18. Everyone, literally *everyone*, in my family unwillingly follows in his footsteps because genetics is such a heartless bitch. If the signs of aging alone defined potential, then I've been a lost cause since before I graduated from elementary school. That is 50 shades of fucked up.

I've previously mentioned the milestone chart that was created for babies when I wrote about "the gap" in the amount of responsibilities between young adults who are the same age. If you cannot recall, I stated that if there was a milestone chart for young adults that told us when we should finish school, get married, have babies, have a career, or otherwise, then we'd all need a one way ticket to the nearest shrink's couch. Here's the problem—there kind of *is* a chart. It's not an official one, but society has made *damn* sure that we know that there is a heavily implied one.

That implied chart is why everyone is in a rush ALL the time. We always feel like time is running out, and the only reason we feel that way is because we have convinced ourselves that we have to accomplish "big things" and "be established" as young as possible. Yet at the exact same time, we look to adulthood with dread in our eyes because we fear falling into a life of continuous monotony. We want everything and nothing at the same time.

The problem with this viewpoint (and the implied chart) is that it's not realistic for a lot of people due to various reasons, yet we've all become convinced that we should be living that way. Quarter life crises are occurring more often, and the suicide rate for all groups have been increasing over the past few years. Depression and anxiety won't be upstaged to that new "crisis" bitch though. As it turns out, approximately 1 in 20 Americans age 12 and over reported that they are currently suffering with depression—*age fucking 12.* (This is all according to the CDC, by the way.)

If we took the time, that we don't believe we have, to sit down and think about how unreasonable the strict time limitation we've put ourselves on really is, then perhaps things wouldn't seem as gruesome. In fact, maybe we'd be happy, because we'd be pissing on ourselves from laughing at how ridiculous it all really is. Let's think about it for a few moments.

According to society, you're supposed to plan out your entire career path between the ages of about 14 through 16 while you're in the first half of your high school career. This way, you'll have the time to plan out what classes and activities to enroll in during your junior and senior years so that you stand a good chance of getting into the college that you want to attend. This has a prerequisite of knowing what you want to do for the rest of your life already. You still have to ask permission to use the bathroom, and may not be allowed to legally drive a car yet, but you're supposed to be fully capable of making the most life altering decision anyone could possibly make during this time…right, sounds legit.

When you're 17 and 18, you're expected to graduate from high school. Immediately following the ceremony, you're expected to be an automatic, professional adult. You're expected to leave home to go to college, but if you've made the unspeakable decision of staying in state for college, then you had *better* move out of your parents' home, because you're an *adult* now!

I swear, it's like I can hear a group of older adults collectively screaming, "We know that you have all of that money saved up from working weekends and evenings selling frozen yogurt. You *HAD* a minimum wage, part time job for approximately seven whole months! Why the hell aren't you in your own apartment yet! Freeloader! Get a "real" job and be fully independent while you're also in college!"

Age 19 is the year that you're supposed to be a party animal. You've already gotten into the swing of college, so now you can afford to party a bit. Besides, it's your last year of being a teenager, so you better do your last stupid thing while society is still a little forgiving. Let's completely disregard the fact that you cannot legally drink in the US, because your job at this point is to party, get drunk, throw up in weird places, and experiment with substances that no sane human being would put into his or her body. At some point, you're expected to drunkenly get a tattoo that you'll regret. Note, many potential employers will use this tattoo as an excuse to turn you down for jobs because it's "unprofessional," so you better make it a good one.

You're also expected to hook up *as much as possible*. I mean, you better do it until your legs fall off!

Be careful though, you don't want to get a disease, or worse, end up with an unwanted pregnancy on your hands. You only *really* have to worry about pregnancy part (and your reputation) if you're a girl though, because boys will be boys. The male species has absolutely *no* control over themselves nor their sexual desires. It's the female's responsibility to prevent such things because males are nothing more than helpless, animal-like savages who are controlled by their dicks.

If you have managed to party without ruining your life, then by age 20 or 21 you must stop *most* partying. (You may still attend wedding parties, baby showers, and anniversary celebrations, but don't go too crazy while you're there.) I know you may be legally allowed to drink now, but you have to be a grown up, because teenagers are the only group of people who are discovering new things about the world, and are allowed to have fun and make *some* mistakes. You're a twenty-something now, which means that you're perfect, and that you know everything. You find life's complexities to be a laughing matter. You definitely know *exactly* what you want to do with the rest of your life, *all* of it. Every single day that you spend on Earth from this point forward will be lathered in clarity. You've got the shit scheduled to the minute, and it'll all go *exactly* how you planned it. That's how life works, after all.

I hope that you didn't have too much fun at age 19, because if you did then it is possible that you failed a class, and failing would put you behind schedule. You're 22 now, and it is time to graduate college! I know that many universities are struggling to offer every class that is needed for students, but you cannot let something as minor as needing a class that isn't being offered this semester stop you from graduating. You need to graduate *now*, so figure the shit out. If the class that you need is full, then just find the smallest kid in that sucker, and make it look like an accident. You've got a seriously implied milestone chart to comply with—forget your morals!

Once you've gotten that whole undergraduate business out of the way, it's time for the real fun to begin! You're almost 23 years old now, and there are just more hours in the day for you than there are for any other group of people on the planet (or any other rouges that may be hiding elsewhere in the universe). We'll begin by having you immediately enrolled into Graduate School, because you're on a tight schedule that has no room for error, vacation, thinking, or breathing. Once you are registered with your chosen place of education, your next task is to find a job—a *super* adult job too. There will be no more coffeehouses or retail jobs, because those aren't considered "real" jobs, especially now that you're past the age of 22.

Let's be honest, positions of *service* cannot possibly be *real work*. What do you even do all day? Or all evening? Or night? Or on the weekends? Real jobs are only opened Monday through Friday from 9a.m. to 5p.m. With the exception of medical positions, all of those other jobs are *obviously* imaginary because they take place when real workers are off from work. I should also mention that you are still required to have a social life because when you are trying to find your next job you'll need to have multiple connections. You cannot get those if you are doing things like studying so that you don't fail any of your classes, or working so that you can eat.

If you're a real champion, then at the age of 24, you should be finishing up your grad school career. Congratulations! It is time for another job upgrade! Immediately upon graduating, you will walk off of the stage, out of the building, and right into the career that you've been going to school for 20 years to achieve. If you chose to be a doctor, lawyer, or any other profession with longer educational requirements, then you'll just have to be patient. Don't worry though, you'll jump RIGHT into making *major* cash when you are done, and 90% of the time those student loans that threatened to leave you in hundreds of thousands of dollars in debt will literally just disappear. If you are in that other 10%, then you weren't worried at all because you had a full scholarship, so didn't have to shell out a dime to attend school. You didn't even spend money to put gas in your car, food on your table, or for insurance costs. You lucky dog, you had a wonderful scholarship!

Now, at age 25 shit gets real. You're like an *official* adult. You'll go to sleep a mere 24 year old adult-child and wake up a Grade A, certified, professional adult. If you've done life correctly, then you should wake up beside someone, or at least have plans to do that within the next 12 months. That's right—you're getting married if you're not already. This step is crucial, because most girls who are 25 are pretty much already menopausal. Guys, you don't get off easily either. Your little swimmers slow down and decrease with age as well. Besides, in just a few short moments your balls will probably be down to your knees, and you need to have kids well before that happens. How can you run around with them if you're tripping over balls? I mean, surely you've heard fathers complain of that, right? Prevention is the best solution!

You're also responsible for purchasing a home, and it better be *Better Homes and Gardens* worthy. There is no possible way that you'll ever move again this late in your life, so you need to make sure that this is the ONE! Upon acquiring your new home owner status, you need to start your retirement plan. Trust me, you don't have very much time left. If you were more responsible, then you would have started your retirement fund at the fetal stage. You know *you* have to keep up with the cost of living, because minimum wage sure as hell won't. Finally, if you have not done so yet, you need to begin writing your will. As I stated earlier, in most cases you do not have much time left, and you need to have your affairs in order.

By the time you reach the 26 through 28 age range, you only have one new task at hand—you need to have some babies. Why do you think you just got married? I hope you weren't thinking that you would be able to spend a couple of years enjoying your marriage with your significant other. There is no time for such childish fantasies, make a damn baby!

If you *really* want to do things properly, then you'll need to have more than one kid, because the first one will need a playmate. There is no possible way that your kid would *ever* make any friends, so as a loving parent, it is your job to provide your little spawn with one or two buddies. However, do not have more than three babies, because that is excessive and damaging to society. There is no way that you'll be able to properly love four or more children at once, so that means that they'll be neglected and turn into self-sufficient psychopaths who are too independent to function properly in society. Besides, living in such close quarters with other who are around their age may cause them to learn to share, or accommodate other people. Do you want to destroy your kids in this way?

Oh dear, I know this seems sudden, but you're 29 now. This means that you are probably in your last year of healthy life. If you are still wearing clothing that may be interpreted as being remotely sexy by another human, then it is time to stop. Actually, you should have stopped when you became a parent, because parents are twice as old as their chronological age. Ladies, if you had your first kid at 25, then you were walking around the world in shorts that were an entire inch higher than your shin as a 50-year-old! How shameful! You really need to learn to cover yourself up.

Guys, for you, the equivalent of this is a muscle shirt. At almost 30 years of age, surely you have experienced extreme, irreversible, age-related muscle atrophy anyway. There is nothing left for you to show off. You wouldn't buy floss for your dentures, so don't buy muscle shirts for your "arms." Besides, the only people who are allowed to wear these things are teenagers and early twenty-somethings, regardless of physique.

More importantly, this is the time to start completing all the items on your bucket list, well, the ones that you are still able to accomplish in such a fragile state. I know your health is seriously declining at this point. I mean, you're almost *30 years old*. If you can still remember your address, God bless you. You are doing extremely well.

I'm not sure if you retained enough of your cognitive abilities to remember how to count, but I'm sorry to inform you that you're 30 years old now. It is at this point that you will probably lose your physical and cognitive function due to age, and you'll no longer be able to achieve or learn anything. You're so old that *you don't even know what time Taco Bell closes anymore.* Seriously, your life is over.

The good news, however, is that some people do live on to be 35. During the last five years of their lives, they spend time with their children, who manage to make time for their excessively aged parents between studying for college entrance exams, playdates, and nap time. It is never too early to start, you know. Those 35 years go by so quickly that if you don't do everything within the first 20 to 25 years, then you're really looking at a totally lost cause. It's not like the average person in the US lives to be 77 or anything.

Can you imagine that? A place where most people live to be almost 80—or even 70? Hell, 65 would be great! I mean, if people lived to be 65 years old, then that means that they could get married a bit later. They may even have their first kid at the age of 30, or a tiny bit later. There would be time for a career change, and you'd have a bit of cushion if things didn't go quite as planned after college. Who knows, people may go traveling again, or even for the first time. There would be *so* much more we could do if we didn't die at 30 to 35. Well, except wear sexy clothing, because like, ew... You'd be so *old*.

-X

Death

There is one aspect of life that never loses its ability to shift your entire perspective on any given situation, and that's knowing that it will end someday. Death is the sole experience of life that remains relatively untainted by the media, because there is no way to make it appear glamorous enough to trick people into thinking that they covet it. Besides, it will always be an individual experience. No one who has truly experienced death can return to tell anyone what it felt like. Even if someone could return, they still couldn't tell you what death would feel like for *you*. There's no way to truly prepare for that moment, but you know that have to experience it. How is that for a dick move from Mother Nature?

Most of us confront death for the first time when we lose a grandparent, or someone else of the older generation. It is a mind bending experience to try to convey to your brain that someone who used to exist doesn't exactly exist anymore. No matter what you do or where you go, you can no longer experience their presence with any of your five senses. It's like you've become selectively blind, deaf, anosmic, ageusic, and numb to nothing except them. That person may have died, but you're the one who feels broken.

Death in the older generation is unpleasant. It's an electrifyingly painful experience to all of those who share a bond with that person, but the fact is that deep within our psyche we expect it. As humans, we have a terrible habit of trying to make immensely complex situations extremely simple, and death is no exception. In our minds, we envision life as progressing in a linear fashion of: birth, childhood, young adulthood, adulthood, being elderly, and then death. However, that is wishful thinking in its most desperate form. The reality is that not every pregnancy results in a life, sometimes old people get *extremely* old, and as I learned a few years ago, not every teen grows into an adult.

It is not a secret that I've never been very good at communication, social events, or making friends. I've accepted that I will never master those things. (Ergo, the reason that I'm writing within a virtual world filled with strangers, and I *still* have to remain anonymous in order to express myself.) However, through a supernatural combination of luck and circumstance, I did manage to make one very close friend a few years ago. We were such opposing forces that it should have been completely impossible for us to tolerate being in the same building without repelling from each other, but we became best friends. United by the harsh realities of being misunderstood and prejudged due to medical histories and arrest records, the book nerd and the reform school dropout formed a bond that was like an oasis in the desert that we knew as social acceptance.

For the next two years, I spent the majority of my time feeling like every social problem that I'd ever faced was solely because I was around the wrong people my entire life. The inability to eat lunch in the cafeteria because too many people were in the room didn't exist when we ate together. The unwillingness to talk on the phone because I'd become drenched with nervous sweat didn't exist during our three hour, late-night conversations. Most surprisingly, my absolute refusal to visit a school event went out of the window when he wanted to go as well.

I'd finally found the right person. He was such a captivating ray of light that I became blind to the darkness that used to surround me. It was literally impossible for it to exist in his presence. I'm not going to get into the details of our friendship. It is far too personal to share, even through this veil of anonymity. It's a permanent secret between the two of us, because I won't tell anyone, and he cannot.

There are a few things that I know to be truth; things that I could never forget even if someone removed my brain from my body. The first is that string beans are an invention of the devil. The second is that my mother is my hero. The final one is that the moment that I got the phone call telling me that the only person whom I ever wanted to be near was permanently taken away from me in a car crash was the worst moment of my life.

It didn't make any sense to me. How the hell was it that with all of the people in this world, the driver managed to hit the car with *him* in it? There are literally *millions* of people in the world with *multiple* friends who are out in modern society and all of its dangers every day, yet this driver collided with the car that was carrying the *one* friend I'd ever truly cherished. I wouldn't wish death upon anyone, but I desperately wanted to wish it away from him. I don't know if that makes sense, but quite frankly I don't care. I just want my friend back.

You know, I want to be grateful that I finally felt it. I know what the human connection feels like because I was privileged to have met him. I understand why other people crave it so desperately, because I crave it now too, but I only want to talk to the person whom I cannot talk to. I miss someone who cannot do anything about me missing him. Even if we both wanted to visit, there's no way for him to return from wherever it is that he is now. How the fuck is this possible, and what the hell am I supposed to do about it?

There are too many unanswered questions that speed through my mind just as quickly and dangerously as the car that took his life. They rush along the overcast roads of my psyche, causing my heart to accelerate to incomprehensible speeds before they collide with each other every time a familiar moment plows through my floodgates and sends me recklessly scurrying down memory lane. Does he still exist? If he does, then where is he? I know he was here because he's in my pictures, so he has to be *somewhere*. Can anyone tell me where he is, exactly? No? Then maybe he just doesn't exist anymore. Great, so I miss someone who technically isn't real now? People think that I'm crazy anyway, but this has *got* to be the final straw.

It is said that there is a lesson to be learned in every tragedy, but I cannot untangle myself from the chains of anger long enough to find the wisdom in this. Seriously! What was the point of finding the one thing that I've always needed, then having it taken away right before one of the most confusing times in my life? Why take him away from me when I need him the most? The years have slowly rolled pass me, and it still doesn't make any more sense than it did the night that I was given the news.

People say that nothing lasts forever, but heartache is proving to be invincible. It doesn't matter how much he'd want me to move on. It doesn't matter that I know he'll never come back. I can't forget someone who drastically changed my life. I can't afford to forget the person who taught me that acceptance and worth are not dependent upon each other, because society's outcasts can still be the hero of someone else's story. His death is one of those things that no amount of therapy will ever correct in my head. He may be invisible to everyone else, but even death can't break our bond. He's in every inkblot that they show me.

We live life with death constantly kept in the peripheral view, pretending that if we don't look at it, then it won't look at us. However, if there is one thing that becoming a young adult has taught me it's that the inability to cope with something never makes that thing go away. (In fact, you may start seeing it everywhere you look.)

The existence of death cannot be erased from our lives. We acknowledge it all the time in little ways that come to us cleverly disguised as ordinary moments. Childhood ends. We graduate and leave school. Friendships end. People breakup. We change jobs. All of these are little tastes of death. We spend every second of our lives dying, it's just that some moments are more clearly defined than others.

Our lives are our stories. We have the power to make them just about anything that we want them to be, but no matter how good the story is, eventually, it has to end. We have no say when it begins, and we never know when we're writing on the last page. The only choice we have in the matter is whether or not we keep fighting to write a good story.

A lot of us are destined to be novels while some of us are novellas, but the fact is that some of us may be novelettes, or maybe even a short story. We have no idea where we land on the spectrum until the story is over, and someone else is inscribing our back cover so that the world has an idea of who we really were beneath all the stereotypes and misconceptions. I had the honor of being a part of the best short story that I have ever read, but having to write the blurb on the back cover is like putting a piece of me in the grave—uncomfortable, scary, and panic-inducing. However, it needs to be done. He deserves it.

I hope you like your back cover, Dude. It's forever a part of my story, just like you. Thanks for being awesome.

-X

Growing Up
(The Shit No One Tells You)

As we grow older, we are bombarded by people who love to tell us things like, "You're too old to [insert whatever activity you really want to do] now." We live in a world where we are demographics before we are human. The first world's favorite pastime is not playing baseball, partying, or going to concerts—it is advertising. The economy doesn't work if we don't buy things, so companies will stop at *nothing* to persuade us to purchase their product. This is done is by targeting people of a certain gender, race, or age group (age group being the most influential), and making them feel like a product was made specifically for them, and no one else.

Merchandise is typically created with a static age range in mind. The problem is that humans are not stationary creatures. We age continuously. However, age doesn't necessarily change what we like as individuals, and that creates tension between what demographics say we should like, and what we actually like. Modern society doesn't like disorder, so the solution is to paint a very detailed picture of what each age group should resemble. If we don't blend in with that image, then we are viewed as being either too immature or too boring, and the things that once brought us enjoyment are now considered our "guilty pleasures."

Age has become a time bomb that is always slowly ticking away in the corner of our minds, awaiting the moment that it should detonate and annihilate our ability to freely enjoy the things in life that make us happy. We've become convinced that its purpose is to completely dictate our hobbies, energy levels, beauty, and ability to learn or try new things. The older we get, the less we are worth, at least according to society and its commercials. We became afraid of getting older, because the world that we live in gave us reasons to fear it.

At some point, usually between the ages of about 16 to 26, we start freaking out about how big the number is getting, and we want the whole growing older thing to stop. Time is going by too quickly, and there wasn't enough of it in the first place. We don't want to be responsible for bills, taxes, caring for homes —and *oh my God*, life is going to be so damn boring!

Our entire lives, we're led to believe that we need to hurry up and become teenagers, but then never age past 29— 27 if we can help it. It seems like every article related to being an adult is someone talking about how boring it is, or how much it sucks. We've given other people's idea of age such a powerful position in our lives that we don't seem to realize that being bored is a choice. If someone else's adulthood is boring, then perhaps that person is just a hopelessly boring individual. It doesn't mean that we have to follow in their footsteps. We do have *some* say in our lives.

I don't know if anyone else realizes this, but we're allowed to do great things past the age of 29. I know this because my father is in his 50's and he is traveling for the first time. My mother's friend is in her 40's and she just became a mom for the first time. My neighbor is 35, and he and his wife were having water gun fights in their yard last week. I could go on with these examples, but I think you get the point. For the first time, I'm starting to notice adults doing things that I previously thought would come to an end once I was "too old" to do them, and it has changed my entire outlook on life.

I wish someone had told me that being an adult is not like the movies make it out to be, or even like our childhood minds make it out to be. In fact, there are *plenty* of things that I wish someone would have told me about growing up that no one bothered to say, so I'll tell them to you in the hopes that I can save you some of the time that I spent trying to figure this stuff out.

I used to think that once I was an official adult I would do the same thing every day until I just retired or died, and let's be honest, these days it's a lot easier to die than to retire without going broke. In reality, life changes constantly. There is no such thing as settling down into life, because life will unsettle us whenever it damn well pleases. We might be fired from the job that we planned on keeping for the rest of our working lives. We might become sick with a serious or chronic illness. We might win the lottery. Hell, aliens might come to Earth. Literally, *anything* can happen. Infinite monotony is only our destiny if we strive for it, but even then, we'll most likely fail.

I wish someone had told me that once I was old enough to do the things that I wanted to do as a kid, I probably wouldn't want to do them anymore. Additionally, if by some chance I did still want to do that thing, then I'd most likely be too broke to do it. I've also overheard multiple classmates citing being too tired as a reason for not doing things as well, but I haven't experienced this yet. I think I could kick eight-year-old me's ass in an endurance competition. (Maybe that's the upside of being anxious all the time, I have lots of energy!)

If you have a childhood dream that still appeals to you, that's great. You should go for it. However, when it comes to things like wanting to watch TV all day, or wanting chocolate syrup for breakfast, you may just grow out of it. Likewise, you may have had a dream career in mind, only to analyze the requirements through an adult's eyes and realize that it isn't right for you. I wish someone had told me that it was normal to change my mind like that. I wish I'd known that we cannot always stick to a plan, or that in most cases, its better not to try to plan out five to ten years of our lives at a time.

I guess I shouldn't have needed someone to tell me that I could not possibly see that far into the future, but so many people have five-year plans that I thought it was abnormal NOT to have one. However, is it *really* normal to plan *everything* out for five years at a time when we don't even know how we'll feel tomorrow morning? I really wish someone had told me that flexibility is required for a healthy outlook on life.

Speaking of those five and ten-year plans, I wish someone would have told me that even if I did have one that I followed perfectly, things could still go wrong. Looking back on it, I'm amazed that my peers and I didn't realize this earlier. We were naive enough to believe that the only people who didn't succeed in life were the people who didn't plan ahead, or the ones who developed an addiction problem of some sort. No one ever sat us down and told us that we were making those plans for fun because life was going to do what the fuck it wanted with us anyway. It's a sucker punch to our comfort to acknowledge that there are adults in this world who had childhood dreams, and those dreams *never* came true due to no fault of their own. Like death, it makes us too uncomfortable, so we just don't mention it.

Perhaps it's because I've had "The American Dream" propaganda drilled into my mind since my brain was still developing in utero, but I swear to you it never occurred to me that my life could end before I found my happily ever after. It seemed impossible, or like a tragedy that could only happen to someone far away, then I lost someone that I cared about. He was supposed to have his entire life ahead of him to make his dreams a reality, but that didn't end up happening. Even if we all live a full lifespan, other things may prevent our dreams from coming true, such as illness, financial problems, or a lack of talent.

If someone had told me this as a kid, then I wouldn't have wasted two years of my damn childhood dreaming of being a cashier, simply because I wanted to push the buttons on the cash register. By those standards, my life dream was made into a reality during the summer that I got my first part-time job, but I didn't particularly like that reality. That brings me back to the point that someone really needs to fucking tell us that we may grow up to dislike the things that we dreamed of as kids, and that we should have a few backup ideas.

I wish someone would have warned me that ending friendships could feel like carving out a piece of my heart and giving it to someone who doesn't even want it. Everyone failed to mention that sometimes two people just stop having things in common. They don't necessarily hate each other. They didn't have a legitimate argument. They just ran out of things to talk about. Life is a journey, and like a car going across the country without stopping, they ran out of gas along the way. Sometimes the distance between the car and the nearest gas station is so great that they're too overwhelmed to remember to say goodbye, so they just leave the car behind and hitchhike in opposite directions to continue the adventure with someone else.

I also wish that the heart came with a warning label stating that it malfunctions sometimes. No one told me that I could feel as though I got divorced when I was rejected by someone I wasn't even dating yet. Do you know all of those awesome feelings you feel when you find "the one?" Yeah, someone needs to mention that you're *ALWAYS* going to feel like you've found "the one" when you initially meet someone you're interested in.

Crushes are exciting because you really think that you've solved a piece of your life's puzzle. It *always* feels right, even when it's *completely* wrong. There is one of two things going on here: Either that whole blurb about how I'll feel the moment I find "the one" is bullshit, and there is no such thing, *or* I just haven't found "the one" yet, and there is a feeling out there that I have yet to experience. The optimist in me hopes that it's the second one, but I have a hefty set of doubts at this point.

Speaking of romantic love and things of that nature, I wish that someone had told me that it was okay not to want those things in my life. It is not mandatory to get married and have kids. I spent a lot of time worrying about if I'd ever be mentally capable of handling the rigors of maintaining a relationship and being responsible for kids, but then one day between life crises I realized that I didn't *have* to do those things if I didn't want to do them. The choice is mine, and I can choose not to partake in those things.

That leads me to another thing that I wish someone, *anyone*, would have told me about growing up, which is that it would only be okay to be myself when the person I was being was consistent with who society wanted me to be. The adult world has bullies just like middle school does, and those people may be someone we have to be in constant contact with. It may be our boss, a coworker, or a stranger on the street who feels the need to say something mean to us. Society will not hesitate to try to crush us because it's only "okay" to be ourselves if society approves of it. If someone had told me this, I'd have a list of prewritten comebacks in my pocket.

Someone should also mention that there are levels to this adulthood thing, and that at some point society will tell us that we're too old to do almost everything that we love, and that we're too young to do everything else. I was vastly unprepared the first time I tried to use my "I'm an adult" card, only to find out that some people who have been adults longer than others don't seem to respect the newcomers. Perhaps that is with good reason, but I cannot say for sure. I know that as a young adult I spend a lot of time confused and making mistakes, but professional adults seem to be majorly confused about one thing in particular, and that's whether or not young adults are *actual* adults or just older children.

When we do something that's legitimately stupid we're told that we're adults who should have known better. We need to get our shit together, pronto. We cannot get away with such things anymore. We can no longer have innocent fun because it's immature, and we should have left those things behind years prior.

However, as soon as we want to pursue a dream or something of that nature, we're immediately told that we're too young to do those things. We're expected to get well paying jobs, but those in charge of hiring insist that we're too inexperienced, and no one else seems to take us seriously. Well, which is it? I don't particularly care what someone says about me one way or the other, but I'd like for them to get the story straight. Professional adults, either we're in the adulthood club or we're not. You cannot decide which one it is based on your own convenience.

While we're on the topic of jobs and money, did you know that $1,000 is *a lot* of money? Did you know that $1,000 is also *not* a lot of money? I learned this a year or so ago. It takes forever and a day (plus a little bit longer) to make $1,000. It takes even longer than that to *save* a thousand dollars. It does not take very long to spend a $1,000. In fact, if your car breaks in the right spot, you may need a *couple* thousand dollars. I never hated the word 'transmission' until I learned the hard way that a rebuilt one cost about $2,500. I'm at the old, used, beat up car stage in my life. My car's model is never in the same decade as the one we're currently living in. That means that if something on my car needs a $2,500 repair, then I might as well just get a new car. I'd probably end up paying less than I would on repairs.

The harsh reality is that you're lucky if you even *have* a car. I'm one of the few of my classmates who does, and I only have one because it was a gift. I know that as children we thought that by this point we'd be in penthouse apartments, driving $40,000 cars, and wearing designer clothes, but I'm afraid that will have to wait. We have dollar store steaks that we have to borrow money for first! Yes, there *is* such a thing. No, I do not want to talk about it.

It is around this time that I started to wish that someone had warned me that the medical community is actually just another business. I use the term business very lightly. It's more of an extortion method. This is definitely not true for all doctors and other medical professionals, but the majority of the ones whom I have had the misfortune of meeting was in it solely for the money. That crap on TV about how the hospital will treat you like family is the biggest, most misleading appeal to your emotions that I've ever seen in advertising.

My family would *not* charge me $20 for a single aspirin. My family would *not* charge $15 for Kleenex, because I blew my nose twice in the emergency room. Have you ever seen an itemized list of what and how much hospitals are charging the patients in the United States? I want to say that I wish someone had warned me about this, but I'm really glad that they didn't because I would have had a legitimate nervous breakdown when I lost my insurance coverage.

The good news is now you can stay on your parents' insurance plan until you're 26 years old…the bad news is that your parents have to be able to *afford* insurance in order for you to do that. If neither of those things apply to you, then get ready to be considered "private pay." That's when you pay the bill in full with your own money. One half mile ride in an ambulance cost me $1,000 (how ironic), so just try not to breathe around any humans, okay? Above all, stay away from kids! They are germ factories. You *will* get sick and convince yourself that it's totally reasonable to spend $50 on a tongue depressor if it means you can later get a shot of anything that'll make the pain go away.

No one tells you that this life will punch you, *hard*. It'll sock you right in the center of your face, knock you to your knees, and allow you to stand up just long enough so that it can punch you again. You're not safe on the ground either. If you don't get up, it'll literally just kick you while you're down. Life can be a bitch like that. It's around this time that's you'll start doing crazy things, like admiring your parents. Okay, your parents probably told you this one (mine did), but you didn't believe them. It's true though!

I once read somewhere that nothing bonds people together like the knowledge of a common enemy. Well, guess what? One day, you'll realize that life is kicking your parents' asses as well as yours, and you'll begin to bond over it. Pretty soon, you'll find yourself acting *just* like them, and that isn't a bad thing. If your parents made it this far, then you can too. After all, you're basically just a copy and paste version of both of your 'rents. (That's totally how babies are made, right?)

It doesn't have to be all bad though, and that's another thing that no one tells you. I'm sick of adulthood being painted at this picture of never-ending suffering. Truth be told, if you can read this, then you're probably living on the more advantageous side of life. I know that doesn't make you feel better about your personal problems (and it shouldn't), but it's something that no one tells us unless we are being criticized for feeling negative things, and being told to "suck it up." I just want to remind you that there *are* good things about adulthood, even if we don't acknowledge it all the time. No one ever spends the evening talking about how wonderful the good things in their lives are. People only seem to gather to talk about their problems. I cannot tell you what your good things are, but I can tell you that you need to find them and focus on them sometimes.

Life can be hard. Yes, there will be unpleasant surprises throughout the trip, but what no one ever tells you is that it's *supposed* to be like that. Even fairy tales have disappointments before the end of the story; otherwise, there would be no story—not a good one anyway. Life isn't singling you out. We all have a struggle at some point. No one ever told me that, but I was lucky enough to learn it on my own. However, you cannot say the same anymore, because you've officially had your fair warning.

I just gave it to you.

-X

THE REAL WORLD

Made for You

During the years before young adulthood, it seemed like everything on television or the radio was *amazing*. Okay, maybe not *everything*, but there were multiple musicians and television shows that I not only loved, but also found myself slightly obsessed with. At some vague point in time after age 14, there was a drastic shift in my entertainment experience. It seemed like half of everything that I saw was extremely stupid, and the other half just wasn't worth my precious time. There were too many other things that I could have been doing instead of watching mindless programs— like studying, working out, picking up an extra shift, or sleeping.

When this day arrived, I realized that there were two possible reasons for my newfound disinterest in entertainment. The first possibility was that I was actually becoming more mature, and outgrowing the "childish" things that used to fill my days with pleasure. The second possibility was that quality entertainment no longer existed. There was no good music. There wasn't anything on television that wasn't annoying, and clothes were fucking ugly everywhere I turned. It obviously couldn't be ME, right? It was just that every creator in the world hit a rut at the same time, and it left me bored and uninspired…right?

Well, guess what?
It was both.

I'm going to go ahead and make an educated guess that it would be hard for anyone, not just me, to connect with a song about seeing their crush standing up next to their locker when in reality they're single, unemployed, and no where near middle school age. There are absolutely no similarities between that song and their actual life. That doesn't necessarily mean that the song is bad, but it's probably highly uninteresting to *that* person. The obvious solution would be to find something that is more relatable to their lives and current situation. There is just one slight problem: practically every new entertainer is approximately 12 years old or under.

There seems to be a very limited amount of new creative projects aimed at people who have passed through their teen years. Hell, after our twenties are over we may as well not even be able to see or hear because there is practically nothing (mainstream) made to inspire our creativity. *WHY?* WHY IS THIS! I'm not really sure of what the answer is, but I think it has something to do with sucking the hope out of people before they realize that they still have a chance to do something amazing.

That isn't to imply that teenagers and tweens cannot do great things, but we seem to forget that people *over* the age of 29 can as well. At this point, I'd probably say that if I see one more product made specifically for young adults I'd scream, but I think I'm in the middle of writing one.

I promise that I didn't do this intentionally. It's just that I *am* a young adult. However, I'm feeling all of those stereotypical 40-year-old feelings already because most of the new things that I'm seeing are geared toward "tweens." I do not relate to most of it, and I just cannot tolerate the rest.

I'm not fascinated with who is wearing what, or who is dating who. I don't care about having the latest phone or smart watch. I never cared about those things, but at least when I was a tween, I could just avert my attention to one of the other five billion things that were being created for my entertainment (and possibly my destruction). There is no such luxury as a young adult. It's like we transform from normal humans who like music and movies, to uninspired workaholics who only need to see content about lawsuits, insurance policies, and tax return services. The fucking ads that are currently on my browser's side bar are for denture cream and online dating—neither of which I looked up or have any interest in.

It never made any sense to me how companies marketed so hard toward kids, when the adults are the people with the money. Is it because kids are more likely to see or believe the advertisements? Perhaps, but whether they believe it or not doesn't matter if their parent refuses to buy the product for them. However, in defense of the tweens, this statement will probably also apply to those in their 30's soon, because with the current job trend we'll probably still be depending on our parents a little bit (or a lot bit) at that point anyway. I know you probably think I'm joking, but I've been out there in the "real world." I am *NOT* joking. It's like a bottomless pit of disappointment out there.

My point is that companies need to expand their horizons and market to other age groups. It's not like they aren't capable of selling us shit too. They sold college extremely well to both young adults *and* our parents, and college is only truly useful if you're trying to become one of approximately three professions.

There are people older than 12 in this world, and we're sick of this shit. A company's lack of ability to recognize that millions of us fall between the ages of training pants and denture cream does not reduce our need for entertainment and inspiration. Our creative sides need to be nourished just like they were when we were children. We need to be reminded that we're never too old to give birth to new ideas.

We are more than the implications of our age, gender, and race. We are living clay. Each day of our childhood is spent revolving around life's table as the agile hands of art and imagination mold us into individual shapes. However, this process doesn't end when the table stops turning. It ends when the fire has sealed us into our final form and we go on to become stationary pieces left on display to inspire others. It is a human need to be able to reach out and grab a little taste of inspiration. We need to experience something that brightens the darker days, but also showcases the beauty of breakdowns. Sometimes art is the only hope we have in the world. We'll spend our entire lives creating our pieces, and I just hope that the supplies are there when we reach for them.

-X

Songs That Someone Needs to Write for Young Adults:

1. I'm so Confused
2. Running Out of Money (Before I Run Out of Bills)
3. I Feel so Old
4. I Hate My Job (And My Boss…And My Coworkers)
5. Monday Again (Already)
6. Love (I Will Never Find It)
7. I'm Still Confused
8. I Can't Find a Job
9. Ramen Noodles (They're What's for Breakfast…and Lunch…and Dinner)
10. The Weekend (Is too Damn Short)
11. This Isn't What I Wanted (Order Me a New Life)
12. No Mom, No Grandkids This Decade
13. Late Fees (Thou Art An Evil Bitch)
14. Time (I Need More of It)
15. Kids (They're Worse Than I Ever Was)
16. Where is My Coffee?
17. The Confusion (Will Never End)
18. Tomorrow Will Be Just Like Yesterday
19. I Don't Have Medical Insurance (Please Don't Infect Me)
20. Regrets (Almost Everything Back to the Fetal Stage)

School vs the World

I used to think that if I performed well in school, then I would automatically be very successful in the "real world." However, that isn't always the case, because there is a disconnect between what is taught in school and what we actually need to know in order to be hirable, independent, functioning adults in society. There is an ocean of misinformation in the world about the ways in which education will benefit us, so let me clarify this for you now.

First of all, *please* let go of the idea that having straight A's on each and every report card will somehow benefit you once you're an adult. The honest truth is that it won't do much for you; I'm sorry. I've filled out countless job applications, and none of them asked me for my final grade point average. *However*, all of the applications asked what was the highest level of education that I had completed. It doesn't matter whether or not you have a 4.0 GPA, you just have to finish. I really wished someone would have told me that. Instead, everyone perpetuates this perfectionist way of thinking that leads to worrying about the number aspect of our grades, more than on *actually learning* the information being taught—which screws us over more than it helps us.

I know you're bored in school. I was bored in school. Everyone is bored in school, but we're told to go because we need an education. What I don't understand is that if we're going to sit through something that we don't want to do because we want to have a beneficial reward for our future, then can it *actually* be beneficial, please? Sure, employers require educational documents, but most of the damn education itself is just not useful to the average person, or even the above average person. Most of it is only truly useful in the confines of the school and other academically oriented environments. I have lived plenty of typical days as a young adult, and not one time have I ever needed to graph a fucking polynomial function. I never needed to find the volume of a cube in order to progress onto a new level of independence. I *definitely* never needed to recite the Krebs Cycle to anyone in a job interview. I don't even remember how to do most of this stuff anymore, and I was an honor student.

History may be important, but our current government is so useless that all history lessons will do now is further piss you off when you realize how much of a joke we've become. Not to mention, the general population is so misinformed about how the government actually works, that I'm pretty sure they chose not to pay attention in this class anyway. It is the one thing that would have helped them in real life (other than English class), and it seems as though no one paid attention. Wonderful.

School does a fantastic job of giving us information that makes us sound smarter, but isn't extremely useful because it doesn't help us to function in our day to day lives. Like, I know that the lines on the road are parallel lines, but that doesn't help me to drive any better. I found an old report card with a note from the teacher telling my parents that I needed to work faster because I wasn't picking up chemistry as quickly as the other students, and I also took too long on the exams. Well, teacher who shall not be named, another year has gone by and would you look at that— I still haven't found the need to use stoichiometry in my daily life. What a total and complete shock!

The worst part about it is that if school is trying to prepare us for the "real world," then it is preparing us to be totally incapable of surviving on our own. School teaches us to follow the rules so well that it leaves us reliant on others for direction. We literally cannot go into a private area to partake in a basic biological function, known to the general population as pissing, without permission from a teacher. We also have to get a note from that teacher so that the other hall administrators know that it's "okay" for us to be there.

We also cannot eat when we're hungry; we have to eat when they tell us it is time to eat. Everything about school teaches us to ignore our body's natural biological clues, which we are supposed to be attuned to, in favor of obeying rules created by another human. After years of always listening to others, they'll toss us out to the world and tell us to find our way using our heads—you know the ones we haven't been allowed to listen to for 13 years or more. It's like we know all the parts of a car, but we don't know how to drive and we're are expected to navigate New York City.

This goes hand in hand with the fact that at the ages of 16 through 18, we are being told how much we *don't* know about the world (and in all fairness we don't know much). We are told how we must listen to our parents, teachers, coaches, and the like because the rules are there to help guide us. We are reprimanded for questioning authority, also known as "talking back." (I don't know how the hell you're supposed to communicate without replying, but *okay* professional adults.) However, at the same time, we are expected to be knowledgable enough to plan out our lives for the next five years.

So, let's get this straight: We need to make a decision about our future careers *now*—while we supposedly know *nothing* about world. Then we need to choose a career path, based on reasons that we're *told* are important, and spend tens of thousands of dollars to (possibly) leave our families for four or more years so that we can learn to do this career for a living. Once we've graduated, we're expected to do that one job every day until we die (or retire, but most likely die).

Am I the only one who sees a problem with this? I think this is a problem. How is it that as teenagers we're unable to see certain movies, drink alcohol, or participate in other "grown up" activities because we aren't mature enough, but we're expected to be mature enough to shape the rest of our lives in their entirety? We've only been alive for about 18 years, and we don't even remember the first three of them. This shit is unfair.

Then there's the fact that school teaches us to judge our abilities on a very limited scale. The amount of effort that we put forth is not important (as is evident with being rushed to crap out information on an exam). The only thing that is important is our ability to regurgitate information that we heard during the previous week onto a sheet of paper. School doesn't convey how smart we are, it shows how good of a memory we have. (It also teaches you how long you can hold your pee.)

Not to mention the fact that the grading scale is one of the most unrealistic, fucked up scales that I have ever witnessed in my life. I understand that all schools are different, but my school grades on an eight point scale. This means that we had to puke back 92% or more of the right stuff to receive an "A." This doesn't seem that bad, until you realize that this also means that if we regurgitate 66% or less of any informational chime, then we've *failed*. Yes, we can get more than half of the stuff right and still be considered a failure. If this was the case in real life, then no one working in customer support would have a job.

The fact that school grades us at all is pretty stupid when you think about it. We go to school to *learn* things. I think we'd all learn more if we weren't so stressed out about a stupid grade—especially when that grade is based on unfair details. There are plenty of people in the world who have learned a foreign language without being reminded every six to nine weeks of a trivial number or letter that won't help them to get a job.

However, the worst part is that school teaches us that all things make sense, and the world teaches us that absolutely nothing makes sense. At school the poor kids get free lunch, the slightly poor kids get reduced lunch, and the average kid pays for lunch. In the "real world" though, everyone is expected to pay the same price for their lunch, regardless of how much money they have. Also, in school we'll learn in biology how delicate Earth's ecosystems are, and that we should care for the planet, but in the real world they'll frack the fuck out of the Earth if it means an extra dollar. Everything is about money.

Don't get me wrong, school is not useless. However, it'd be nice if instead of being forced to ~~not~~

~~actually~~ read Shakespeare we were taught how to balance a checking account without being reliant on a computer system. It would be awesome if school taught us how to properly hunt for a "grown up" job, or at least how to create a resumé. We could have all the education in the world, but if we don't know how to market ourselves then we don't reap any of the benefit.

If school is so important, then why not just look at our school records when determining which applicant to hire? If being a great salesperson is the most important thing, then school should teach us to sell. It is pointless to send us into the world with a pretty piece of paper stating that we know about graphs, chemicals, and old English, if what we really need is a kick-ass sale's pitch. If life was a game, that would be cheating!

School? Real World? How about you two schedule a meeting on Monday morning to discuss the communication issue at hand? It is causing a rapid breakdown in the young adult community, and it seems that you have not yet taken notice. Please, go do your homework. You're failing right now.

-X

Life Lesson #1
School vs. Employment

What you learn in school

How to spell your name*

What you need to know in order to get hired

*This is usually taught at home before entering school.

Banking

When thinking about growing up, very few of us think about the mundane errands that adults are obligated to perform on a frequent basis. There is the burden of taking your car to get oil changes, laundry, and lawn care. Do you remember those days when the food would just appear in the house? Yeah, those days are over, Buddy. You have to partake in grocery shopping now—which is actually fun until you have to pay for stuff. Most errands are just boring obligations, but then there is banking.

Banking is on an entirely different level than the normal, boring responsibilities that we acquire as adults, because banking is stupid. I'm not kidding. It's literally the stupidest thing that I've ever taken part in, but I never stop because I have been conditioned to believe that I cannot be completely responsible without participating in this task. However, I realized very early on that banks are *not* your friend, and I really wish I knew how to cut that bitch out of my life without hurting my adulthood progress meter.

I believe that my hatred is well justified. For example, let's say that you have $700. You're trying to be a responsible adult, so you put that money into a checking account. Awesome! You're on your way to greatness. You have bills to pay, so do that. P*ay* those bills! Now, you probably have about $100 left in that checking account of yours. Actually, if you're a young adult, then you probably don't have $100 in your account. You probably don't have *anything* in your account. In fact, if you're really being typical here, then you probably have less than nothing in your checking account. Yes, I'm talking about those negative numbers that you were introduced to in algebra. Those numbers that you didn't think you'd ever need in "real life" because there was no such thing. Oh, you need them, because those imaginary fuckers are *all* you have. School was hinting at us from the beginning that it wouldn't make us rich, but we failed to read between the lines. We brought this on ourselves.

Anyway, so you have $100 or less in your account. This is where the fun begins, and it comes in the form of service charges. First of all, you probably get charged anywhere from $8 to $12 per month for simply having that account. Yes, you have to pay someone to let them hold your money. Who doesn't like to hold money? However, that is understandable, I mean, businesses have to make money some way. Okay, we'll give them that one.

Now remember, you have less than $100 in your account. Guess what? You better get ready to receive another service charge! Why? Well, because banks have this rule that states that you have to have a minimum amount of money in your checking account, or you'll receive a service charge. (At my bank, the minimum is actually $500, but I'm trying not to be excessively depressing here.) I don't know what this service charge is actually called, but I call it the "You're broke, Asshole" fee. That's right. You just got charged for being broke, because that makes sense.

It wouldn't be true adulthood if the fun stopped there. For the sake of argument, I think it is safe to say that if you're being charged the, "You're broke, Asshole" fee, then you don't have as much money as you need to live comfortably. That means that you've probably over drafted your account at least once. This is where those imaginary numbers come in. You have less than $0 in your bank account because you owe the bank money. If you're anything like me, then it may be the "You're broke, Asshole" fee that caused you to fall off the financial cliff. In any case, guess what? You win another service fee!

I know for a fact that this is called an overdraft fee. Basically, you were so broke that your number of dollars took a vacation at the negative number resort. The bank thinks that the remedy to this is simply to charge you more money. Now, you have a bigger negative number. Did you overdraft by $2? Well, you don't have -$2 in your account, you have approximately -$32 in your account, because being broke is the most expensive thing that you can be.

At this point, you're probably thinking that this whole banking thing is not for you, and I don't blame you. I had the same thought. So, you probably paid the fees—if you have direct deposit enabled, then it may have automatically been taken cared of for you when your check was deposited into the account—and you are probably thinking of cutting your losses now by just closing the account. I have a surprise for you. You win another service charge! I'm not sure if all banks do this, but at the first bank that I went to I was charged a fee to close the account. I literally had to pay them to take my own money back.

In case you're having a bit of trouble keeping up, I'll summarize it for you. You acquired some money, and tried to be responsible by putting it in the bank to keep it safe. You handed a complete stranger your money, and they charged you for letting them hold it. Then, if at any point they decided that you didn't give them enough money to hold, they charged you *more* money. If you were too poor to pay that fee, they fixed that by charging you another fee. When you finally had enough of that losing game, and tried to take your money out of their hands completely, they charged you *another* fee. I think that last one is called an "account termination fee," but I like to call it "bullshit." You shouldn't have to pay someone to take back the pitiful amount of money that they were charging you to hold in the first place.

Even if you decide to pay all the fees and close the account, there is still the problem of trying to be completely functional in society without a bank account. There are a lot of companies that won't let you use their services without an active checking account. Not to mention that cashing your paycheck begins to cost more than the paycheck is worth, and shopping without a debit card is hard unless you're carrying cash —which isn't safe. I mean, when you're out and about you may run into a criminal. That's the last thing you'd want to happen. You worked hard for each and every dollar that you have in your pocket, so you better keep it in a safe place. After all, if you don't keep it in the bank, someone may come along and steal it. -_-

-X

How I Became Happy about Living with My Parents (The Apartment Story)

When I was younger, the one thing that I always talked about was the glorious day that I would old enough to have my own apartment. I'd been conditioned to believe that it'd be the ultimate sign of being a *professional* at this adult thing.

The perks were endless. I could leave when I wanted. I could come back home when I wanted. I could watch *what* I wanted on TV *whenever* I wanted to watch it. I could stay up all night. I could have junk food for breakfast, and no one would ever know. I wouldn't have to clean up every day if I didn't want to, because I would make the rules. My laundry wouldn't have to be folded, and I wouldn't have to make my bed every morning. The best part would be that my music would no longer be confined to my headphones. I could play the most explicit stuff whenever I wanted! My parents wouldn't live there!

My fantasy didn't stop with the freedom to do what I wanted to do. I dreamed of how I would deck out my apartment. I knew exactly what part of town I wanted to live in—which was *SO* much cooler than the part of town that I currently lived in. I couldn't wait. All I had to do was be old enough to get my own apartment and then the world would be mine!

Do you have to be a genius to figure out that shit didn't work out that way? In case it wasn't apparent from my other posts—shit did not work out that way. Shit didn't even work out half of that way. It's not that the apartment wasn't all that it was cracked up to be; it's that I've never been able to afford one yet. I can't even afford an apartment on the bad side of town, much less the part of town that I dreamed of living in. That's just the first of many realizations that slapped me in the face once I became a young adult.

I know times have changed since I was a kid dreaming of an apartment, so that part isn't *totally* my fault, but seriously, who the hell made apartments so expensive? I realize that I live in a poorer state than most people, so it'll sound like I'm complaining about nothing, but keep in mind that I live in a state that is dirt poor. Our cost of living is not supposed to be an arm, a leg, half of an ass, and one eyebrow, but it *is* for us.

When I began my search for apartments, I started by asking my *slightly* older family members how much it cost them to rent their first apartment, which they did only about eight to ten years before the conversation took place. The answers ranged from $350 to $400, and that was on a fairly decent side of town. The excitement began to bubble in my chest as I sat down to look at my options.

I was in for a rude ass awakening. Somehow the exact same apartments that were $350 per month when my family members rented them were approximately $720 per month now, and that was for one bedroom. Those apartments were the cheapest ones available on any side of town that I didn't think would require me to have a four member security team, a Glock, and a machete for good measure. My dream was already dead, but then I got fired from my shitty job and my dream got cremated. There was no way that I could make this work. My apartment dream was a zombie, and it had devoured my hopes and dreams.

Initially, I felt extremely bitter about the fact that I didn't have my own place. I started feeling like an adult-child. I was an adult that was able to experience all the consequences that children could not, but since I still lived with my parents, so I didn't receive any of the benefits that were supposed to come along with that burden. All I'd done was successfully get older without anything to show for it. Cue depression.

After a while, something happened though. I began to observe my family members who had apartments and I realized something—those apartments were probably the *stupidest* thing that they'd ever done in their lives.

Now, hear me out. This doesn't apply to those of you who had to move away for school, a job, to get out of a bad home life, or to be with your boyfriend or girlfriend. You're smart, apartment yourself away. I'm talking about the people, like me, who wanted to move out just to prove that they were *real* adults. Apartments don't make you an adult; apartments make you broke.

I don't know what it's like in your area, but in my area we cannot purchase apartments, we can only rent them. This means that we would spend at least $720 each and every month to live in a place that would *NEVER* be ours. We'd be throwing the money that could be used for our future homes into a fire pit. This isn't taking into account other bills such as utilities, gas, Internet, cable, phone, and other "necessities." Do you know what that means? That means our asses better be putting in some *serious* hours at work unless we have a roommate who is allowed to split the rent with us. However, most apartment complexes here just charge more if two people live in the apartment. Yes, for the *same damn space*. That's the first sign that this is a way to strictly make money off of people. There is no real concern as to whether or not they are providing a decent, safe home. Money, bitch. *Now*.

You know, I probably could have gotten over their greed if I worked full-time at a job that paid more than minimum wage and didn't have school hours to worry about, but then the next realization hit me. These apartments are only rentals. I wouldn't have been able to deck it out the way I dreamed of doing. Painting isn't allowed. Hell, I couldn't even nail things onto the wall.

Not to mention that 90% of the time renters are stuck with an ugly ass, allergy triggering carpet that they are not allowed to remove because this thing isn't their damn house.

There is a lot that I could put up with, but not being able to make the apartment look like the one I imagined would have effectively ruined my dream just as much as not being able to get the apartment at all. I mean, isn't getting to do all the crazy shit that we said we were going to do as kids the best part about becoming an adult? If we can't do those things, then being an adult is reduced to being a depressing, soul sucking experience—at least for the bucket list creators among us.

By now, I was almost smiling at the fact that I didn't have an apartment. I mean, I wasn't paying over $10,000 a year for a place that would never be mine. A place that I couldn't even deck out the way I wanted to while I would be there, and would also cause me to have to work so much to pay for it that I'd never be home to enjoy it anyway. However, there was one part about the whole thing that still bugged me to no end, and that was the fact that I didn't feel like a *real* adult.

It's true. No matter what I did I felt like I was a child because I still lived with my parents. What drove me even more insane was the fact that I could not figure out exactly why I felt this way. Once we take away the fluff, an adult is actually just someone who can make responsible decisions. Wasn't accepting my financial situation and refusing to obligate myself to an apartment that I couldn't afford a responsible decision? Was not being able to afford an apartment *really* the reason that I still felt like a child? Well, in a way, but there were just as many older adults struggling exactly like I was. The only difference was that I still had parents to help me. I was *lucky*, so why the hell didn't I feel lucky?

I knew why. It was because I had been conditioned to think that my adulthood was something that I could buy and put on display for everyone else to see, like a grand prize trophy. I didn't feel like an adult, not because I didn't have an apartment, but because I was still thinking like a child. I was still using a mindset that someone else put there for me instead of what actually made sense. I was still trying to impress strangers. I felt like the only way that I could be an adult was for everyone to give me their stamp of approval verifying that I had indeed reached my milestone. I was still trying to bring a gold star home from school—nothing had changed except my fucking age.

Then I realized that it was all a bunch of bullshit. Apartments *were* just like the rest of advertising. The sellers would tell us any and everything to get us to do what they wanted us to do. It's just like photoshopped images in magazines; we know they aren't real, but we strive for that level of perfection anyway. We think that if we somehow acquire everything on the list, then we'll finally become "real" adults with a side order of success. However, now I choose to think that being an adult isn't anything that we can purchase, and it definitely doesn't come with chronological age.

It's easy to understand how we could equate becoming an adult with having our own place. First of all, it's what we're taught since birth. Second, it's what's reinforced on television and in movies. Third, most people around us believe it. Hell, you probably believe it. I know I did. It wasn't until I took a humanities class and studied different cultures that I realized in some places, families actually live together their entire lives.

This is called a multigenerational home, and basically three or more generations live under one roof. So like, imagine living with your parents, then imagine your parents living with your grandparents. Would that make your parents less than adults? Do they deserve less respect because the place where they go to sleep at night just so happens to be under the same roof where their parents go to sleep? I don't think that it does. I'm not saying it is okay to be irresponsible and act like a child in the house forever; what I'm saying is that where you live doesn't determine your maturity. It may determine your status, but I think a great sign of maturity is realizing that status is for other people, and sometimes you just have to tell those people to take their opinions and fuck off.

Now I honestly believe that being an adult is about becoming more thoughtful and making better decisions based on what you know instead of what people are telling you to think. Don't get me wrong, I still struggle with that sometimes. I still want my own place someday, but I want it for different reasons.

I don't enjoy messy rooms anymore. I find great pleasure in eating a healthy diet. A job hasn't turned up yet, but I'm sure it'll pay minimum wage when it does anyway. I don't watch television anymore, and loud music is actually annoying. I've earned the ability to come and go as I please even though I live with the people who made me. Apparently your parents will let you grow up even if you live in the same house with them. Who knew?

However, the fact remains that I would still *love* to deck out a place of my own and make it reek of my childhood visions. It is just that now that I am a bit older and wiser, I would prefer to put that time, money, and effort into something that's actually mine—not something I got for everyone else's approval. After all, there's no expiration date on making dreams come true. I didn't set time restraints as a kid, and I don't think I should have such limitations as a young adult either.

-X

The Internet

I thought that I was too young to experience memory loss. Boy, was I ever wrong. It isn't that I forget entire conversations or anything of that nature, but I cannot remember what the hell I used to do before the Internet was a "thing." Did I play games like hide-and-seek? Were playdates invented then, or was it all spontaneous? The only things that I truly remember is homework, food, and video games—but that could also describe my life a year ago, just add in an Internet connection as well. I hear older people saying that my generation "doesn't get out anymore," but in my case, I'm not sure that I ever did. If I did, then I don't remember much of it. I'm not sure how I feel about that.

In my defense, home Internet was definitely already common when I was a little kid. However, in senescence's defense, it's not like we could afford it or a computer at the time. This is a clear example of how the Internet has taken over our lives. I don't mind it 99.9% of the time though. The times that I do mind are a completely different story.

There are so many things that we use the Internet for that I think it'd be hard for anyone to imagine a life without it now. Do you want to listen to music? Internet. Do you want to reconnect with an old friend? Internet. You don't need to wait to watch the news. The news is always there— 'cuz Internet! Afraid of losing valuable photos? Why? The Internet can fix that. I'm pretty sure that soon we'll be able to purchase an item from across the world and have it shipped to us without even leaving our homes—oh wait…

Now, I'm well aware that the Internet is not all sunshine and chocolate. There are times when it does more harm than good, and I acknowledge that. However, I'm almost positive that a grand total of approximately three people would ever want to *completely* do away with the Internet. The rest of us are too deep in our addiction. Oh, you don't believe me? Well, let's do a quick check to see if you have Internet fever.

YOU MAY HAVE INTERNET FEVER IF:

1. You cannot remember the last time you met someone whom you began dating without the Internet being the reason that you two met.
2. You've gotten into a fight with a friend or family member over something that you posted online.
3. You've scared yourself shitless by Googling your symptoms to find out if you were dying or not. Who knew that that leaky nose was actually your brain's fluid draining through your nasal passages? If not for the Internet you'd be flat headed, dry

brained, and *dead*. After all, you initially thought that it was just ordinary snot.

4. You exclaimed with joy when you learned that "Googling" is finally a real-life verb.
5. You don't know any of the local radio stations. (Why bother when you can create your own? Hello, Pandora, Spotify, Grooveshark, etc.)
6. You check your e-mail before you use the bathroom or brush your teeth in the morning.
7. You only form thoughts with 140 characters or less.
8. You've lost one or more friends due to a political or religious post on social media.
9. Speaking of friends, you cannot remember how tall they are because you haven't seen them (if you still have them) in person for so long.
10. You've said "LOL" or "LMAO" out loud, at least one time.
11. You've lost faith in humanity at least three times before lunch because you read the comment section of an article or video.
12. Tell me the last time you went to bed before 3:00 a.m. I bet it was before the Internet was commonplace.

What I can't understand is why some people have such *deep* hatred for the Internet. I mean, I suppose cyber-bullying could account for some of that, but if we're all so anti-social, then I don't see the problem with ignoring people online as much as we do in real life. Then again, I was bullied in real life, so I'm probably biased. Over the past year, I've developed the ability to ignore people so hard that they begin to question their existence—and that's when they're five feet away from me.

Anyway, I agree. We probably spend more time on the Internet than we should, but no one has ever really told us what we should be doing instead of liking every post on Tumblr that makes us remotely chuckle. I'm a problem solver, so I came up with a few things that I think we could do instead of sitting at the computer all day.

1. **Drugs.** We could all be doing drugs. At least we wouldn't be wasting our lives away safely in our homes. I need the excitement of danger, damn it!
2. **Irresponsibly Having Sex.** Mom wants grandkids, doesn't she? I don't know about her, but I always like when the things that I order arrive earlier than expected. I think she'd enjoy it.
3. **Studying.** Let's be honest though. We'll forget all of that school stuff as soon as we stop using it. That usually occurs around the time that we leave school and have to function usefully in society.
4. **Working**. If you're able to find a job, this may be a good one…good luck finding a job without the Internet though. The last six jobs that I applied for

didn't even accept applications or résumés in person. It was Internet only.

5. **Hanging Out with Others.** My parents don't like my limited number of acquaintances when they only know about them via a wi-fi connection. Do they think that they *really* want to meet these humans in person and have them in their home? I'm pretty sure on some days they barely want ME in their home. I'd stop using that one if I were someone's parent.

6. **Eating.** Whom I kidding? That's just about everyone's favorite thing to do while ON the Internet. That is already covered.

7. **Visiting with Family.** I did that once a couple of years ago, and they seemed overly fascinated by how I grew up just like everyone else. However, as grown up as they thought I was, they all felt that I was doing the wrong thing with my life, and felt the deep responsibility to point me in the proper direction. Everyone's direction was different though. It was a strange and confusing experience. I'm not trying to do that one again. I wouldn't recommend this one.

8. **Shopping, discovering new music, paying bills, watching movies, and reading books**—all of these have been taken cared of by the Internet. You don't have to mention those. We've got it.

9. **Exercise.** Well, that already happens 60 minutes a day for me. If it's not happening for you, then 60 minutes less Internet time a day, buddy. You can keep the other 480 minutes though. Those are all for you!

10. **Sleep.** If we slept now, then what would we do in class? Jeez, don't try to fix what isn't broken.

I think I did it. I think I made my case. Nothing is ever 100% good, but nothing is ever 100% bad either. The Internet isn't the enemy. Perhaps the problems that most of us experience online isn't technology's fault, but the fault of the humans utilizing it. My MacBook Pro has never done anything except help me, and it certainly never called me a mean name. A human, however, has done these things and worse, and it would have happened whether or not the Internet was there to assist them. Instead of vilifying an inanimate object, and cussing the Internet for being the source of our problems, perhaps we should point our fingers at the people who are operating it. After all, the first step of fixing a problem is identifying it. Placing the blame on "the Internet" when we should be blaming the bullies, the "catfishers," the pedophiles, and the like, doesn't do *anything* except provide an outlet for responsibility to escape from.

The World Wide Web didn't create a problem, it only trapped it and made it visible for everyone with a basic Internet connection to see. The core of these issues aren't new, we're just being forced to pay attention now. Maybe we should be thankful that such a flaw in our society was exposed on such a massive level, because it takes away the option to remain ignorant of the problems and challenges that our generation is facing. Again, pretending that a problem isn't there isn't going to make it go away; it is only going to make the problem worse. For those who have been harmed, ignorance is not bliss. Ignorance is pain. We are the medicine. It's time to start healing.

-X

Jobs

It's the question that we are all asked from the time that we are old enough to form two word phrases: "What do you want to be when you grow up?" I despise this question for many reasons. The first of which is because it reinforces the idea that once we're grown up we can only be one thing for the rest of our lives. People change careers all the time. The idea that we are stuck with whatever career we choose as teenagers is a big part of the anxiety that we feel about growing up. If you could only eat one food item every day for the rest of your life, wouldn't it be extremely hard to choose what lunch was going to be now that you knew it was going to be lunch *forever*? The reality is that we get to eat more than one dish. Chances are, while we may be in a general field, we'll probably have multiple jobs over the course of our adult life. Whether or not we have a choice in the matter of changing jobs is an entirely different animal.

The second reason that I hate this question is because it leads us to believe that we should automatically know what we want to be when we grow up. Given, there are the freaks of nature who know from age four what they want to be when they are adults, and they actually become those things. That isn't typical. It happens, but most people do not share this experience. I realized this when I met a 42-year-old woman who was in school because she was changing her career and needed new certifications (which goes along nicely with the first point I tried to make). She laughed as she told me, "I can't figure out what I want to be when I grow up." I don't think she realized that she helped to calm a lot of fears that were constantly throwing a tantrum within me.

I also hate this question because when people ask us, they don't bother to tell us that we'll probably have to go through multiple *really shitty* jobs to get to our dream job. (They also don't tell us that once our dream job is our real job it may not be all that we thought it would be, but the only way to know that is to try it. Once again, that's a different story.) This begs me to acknowledge the fact that many of my former classmates are graduating from college only to find that they are holding the *exact* same job that they held throughout their college career—and in some cases, their *high school* career.

It is *HARD* to find a job these days, and I'm at the point where the idea of a career seems laughable. Employers do not make it any easier with their list of impossible, or at the very least unreasonable, requirements. For example, my first job was at a national retail chain. I was paid minimum wage my entire two years on the job—which I don't want to talk about—and I had no degree nor high school diploma.

My duties at this *lovely* establishment included: keeping the place clean, operating the cash register, and showing people where stuff was located. Now, the assistant manager needed a college degree to hold her position. Do you know what her duties were? The *exact* same list as mine, plus making the schedule and going to the bank once a week to make deposits. She didn't even make $3 per hour more than me. Does anyone else think that needing a college degree for those two extra duties and $2.75 more per hour was a bit of an overkill? She must have, because she quit the first chance that she got.

The biggest challenge, however, isn't meeting the requirements on paper, it is acquiring enough *experience* to be taken seriously by the person who is in charge of hiring. That is where my job search (and life) fell apart. No matter where I looked, every job that I found required a year, or more, of experience in whatever field the job was in. Retail, banking, food service, clerical work—I tried them all.

Will someone please explain to me how a person is supposed to gain "relevant" work experience if no one will hire them to gain that experience? Yes, I had a job at a store, but with a gap in my employment the hiring managers don't think that it is "relevant" enough. I'm always noted as "inexperienced" even though I held a job for two years. Therefore, because I don't have work experience, no one will hire me. I can't gain experience because I don't already have experience. It's an intricate cycle of fuckery that I cannot find my way through.

Let's use banking as an example, since I already hate banks. There were multiple jobs available at the banks in my area; however, none were considering applications for the part-time positions unless the applicant had at least one year of experience working at a bank. The full-time, entry level jobs required three to five years of experience. Entry level jobs…*ENTRY LEVEL JOBS*. Go ahead. Let that sink in.

It was at this point that my parents suggested that maybe I should look for a job in a "broader field," which translates into retail or fast food. I didn't know how to tell them that I'd already done that. Remember that gold star I mentioned earlier? I'd pawn that son of a bitch for a dead end job.

There is nothing inherently wrong, despite what some assholes may say, with jobs in retail or fast food. If you have a job in those areas, then do it proudly. You are earning money and learning how to deal with various types of people in society. I know those jobs do not pay enough money to live on, but you can gain valuable work experience at these establishments… unless you're *overqualified*, then you cannot work there at all. You'll have to gain your experience elsewhere. Yes, it came as a shock to me too. Apparently, if you have too many good paper things, like certifications or degrees, then employers of the jobs that don't require previous experience won't hire you because you're just too good at school.

I've been told that the reasoning for this is that it sends a message to the hiring manager that the applicant won't be at the job for long, or that they aren't serious about the position. Do you know what can better tell hiring managers whether or not an applicant is serious about a position? The response that person gives in a fucking interview! Why don't they *meet* with this person, and just *ask* them? Why don't they learn the reasons why that person applied for that job in the first place? If the job market in their area is anything like the one in mine, then I can guarantee them that this person will be at this job for at least a year gaining experience—if given the chance. This brings me to my next grievance, which is the lack of personal interaction.

Can we please meet an *actual* person? Don't misunderstand me; I *love* computers. I am on a computer for at least a few hours a day, but a computer can only give black and white answers when most of the responses are various shades of grey. Sure, employers can see that someone has a college degree, but do they know why that person applied for the job in the first place? No! Perhaps they need a second job to cover healthcare costs, student loans, or both. They may be in the middle of a career change, or going back to school, or a parent who needs a job better suited for someone who needs to be home by 5:00 p.m.—or maybe they just need to gain some fucking work experience, since they cannot find a job due to the fact that they didn't already have one before they came flying out of utero.

The worst part about the whole damn thing is that if you haven't had a job in a long time, then employers are even less likely to hire you—at least, that's what I was told by managers whom I've met. It's time to play the logic game again! Here we go: Susie has been unemployed for a year due to circumstances beyond her control (bad job market, school, illness, fill in your own blank). Susie is applying for a job at Company X. She has all of the qualifications, but the hiring manager will not hire Susie because she doesn't already have a job, or hasn't had one in a while. *Obviously* she's a dumb ass, because she quit her other job and severely cut her expenses in exchange to go to college full-time a couple of years back. You better not hire Susie, because that bitch *really* needs money.

My last job search convinced me that jobs don't exist in the US anymore, because I'm pretty sure that employers want to own you, and that's slavery. I'm specifically referring to the retail field here, because it is the only one that I've ever personally worked in. I never knew this before having that job, but just because a store is opened from 10:00 a.m. to 9:00 p.m. does not mean that various workers aren't there almost 24 hours of the day. My "favorite" was around the holiday season, when a lot of my coworkers and I were on-call for shipments or floor work.

Do you have any idea of what "on-call" really means when you're in retail? On-call means that you can be called into work at 3:00 a.m. to receive a shipment and handle the merchandise accordingly so that it would be on display in time for opening. Thankfully, my on-call hours were during the afternoon because I was in school at the time. However, it was *extremely* annoying to sit around all day waiting to find out if I had to go to work. I couldn't go anywhere because I promise you, as *soon* as I arrived at my destination, my job *would* call me in. It's like they had GPS tracking on my happiness. However, if I stayed home all day then no one would call, and I wouldn't have to go to work.

I could understand being on-call in the medical profession, but retail? Are these shirts running for the border? I did stay late a few times during the winter break, and at 2:30 a.m., unpacking clothes is either the definition of hell or funniest thing that you've ever encountered. There is no in between.

What about if you're lucky enough to get a job? Shouldn't you be happy with life and fairly independent? Well, the answer to that is no. At this point, it is *highly* likely that your job pays minimum wage, which at the moment is $7.25 per hour *before* taxes. Can we talk about how minimal that really is? I won't even mention car notes, apartments, insurance, and other things that are out of your reach if you're the owner of a minimum wage job. (If you have one of these things, then you sacrificed the others, or your parents give you money regularly.)

Let's talk about low priced items. A medium pizza in my area is about $10. If you work a minimum wage job, an hour of your life is not worth a medium pizza, let alone a large pizza. The prepaid phone plan that I had when I got my first cell phone was $30 a month. You would have to work over four hours to be able to talk on that phone for five hours—and that's *before* taxes. I once heard a politician on the news brag about how he paid for his college education with his summer job. Never mind that this was probably before Christ, let's see if this is possible now.

Working full-time at a typical summer job (and for the sake of argument, let's say that you'll have this job year round) will give you $290 a week, that's about $1116 a month before taxes. Tuition alone at my local college is $2,300 per semester, *IF* you're a resident of the state. If you aren't a resident of the state, then it is well over $14,000. A dorm room is about $3000 a semester, and it costs slightly more for your own apartment. You're looking at $500-$750 a semester for books, and that isn't counting class fees and other supplies. Do you like not dying of starvation? That'll be a minimum of $1000 a semester, please. Don't even ask me about a car or gas, because it should be obvious by now that your ass is walking. Are you planning on having a social life? Then I hope you're ready to go to the park or anywhere else that's the affordable price of free. If you can stay in state, stay on your parent's insurance (if they are lucky enough to have it), and not eat too much, then you can spend a semester in college in my town for approximately $6800.

If you don't have a scholarship, and you don't want to take out a loan because of the uncertainty of finding a job, then you can work full-time for just over six months (before taxes that is) and afford four months in school! I'd advise that you start ahead of time though, because if you're in retail, there's no *way* you're getting 40 hours a week. Near the end of my time at my retail job, I was lucky to get ten hours a week, and most of that was after hours during the summer because no one else wanted those shifts.

I'm not saying that it is impossible to make it. I'm saying it is a lot harder than anyone seems to tell us, yet they wonder why so many young people are depressed. It's because we feel like we're fighting a losing battle. Our days are filled with running in circles trying to find our way, or feverishly chasing the carrot being held in front of our faces trying to achieve something. We are never at rest in the competition of life, but no one seems to acknowledge that the game is rigged, or at least missing some vital pieces. The stereotypical thing to do would be to leave you with encouragement as to why it's all bound to work out in the end, but honestly, I'm not entirely sure if that's true. Things have not gotten better for me, and things are getting worse for those who are trying to go to college now. I haven't been convinced yet that things will get better in terms of financial stability, and at this rate I don't know that I ever will be.

-X

Life Lesson #2
Common Employer Questions and Their Translations

What they say: "When are you available?"
What they mean: "When <u>won't</u> you be at my beck and call?"

What they say: "Why is there a gap in your employment?"
What they mean: "Why didn't anyone else want you?"

What they say: "Do you have any questions for me?"
What they mean: "Are you interested in this job?"

What they say: "Why are you interested in this position?"
What they mean: "How soon will you quit?"

What they say: "What's the minimum amount of pay acceptable for this job?"
What they mean: "How little can I pay you? Better be lower than the previous and next person."

What they say: "Are you in school?"
What they mean: "Will you be here less than that other person?"

What they say: "Where do you see yourself in five years?"
What they mean: "Are you planning on one day NOT being my bitch?"

What they say: "Why did you quit your last job?"
What they mean: "How much shit can I throw your way?"

What they say: "Are you willing to work overtime?"
What they mean: "I _really_ need a bitch. Is it you?"

What they say: "What is your dream job?"
What they mean: "How desperate are you right now?"

What they say: "Why should I hire you instead of another candidate?"
What they mean: "Will you kiss more ass than the other applicants? How about harder?"

What they say: "This is a highly coveted position."
What they mean: "Someone that I know personally wants this job. This interview is for fun."

What they say: "How much experience do you have?"
What they mean: "Can I pay you even less for doing the exact same thing as the older guy?"

What they say: "Are you willing to travel? Relocate?"

What they mean: "Does your ass kissing have geographical boundaries?"

What they say: "We'll be in touch."
What they mean: "Forget it! Just forget it, don't even think about remembering it."

Dress Codes

I don't know about you, but I have attended schools that chose to enforce upon their students a rule that causes misery among the free spirits around the world: they created extremely strict dress codes.

During the years of my life that I was supposed to be becoming whom I was meant to be, I was being told who I was through a mandatory uniform policy. This deepened my hatred of school more than the fact that I had to participate in group projects. Uniforms were a personal insult to my creativity. I wasn't even allowed to wear different shoelaces to personalize my ugly uniform. I was forced to go to school each day dressed exactly like my bullies, and we were all forced to go to school dressed like a stereotypical 65 year old. I think that left a scar somewhere.

I couldn't *wait* until I was old enough to decide what I wanted to wear. I wanted to be the sole person in charge of what I looked like each day. I had my heart set on becoming the image that I created of the "adult" version of myself. That version didn't walk around looking exactly like everyone else.

Well, I hate to be the bearer of bad news if you're currently in that position, but you're probably going to feel like that your entire life. In fact, you might feel the angst to a greater extent as the years roll by due to a little thing known as "employee dress codes." When it comes to my personal relationship with dress codes, they hate my "style" as much as I hate their existence. You could say that dress codes and I are in an unhappy, sexless marriage, because we don't fuck with each other.

Please don't misunderstand what I'm saying, because I do believe that *some* basic rules are good. If your *job* requires a uniform, then I can understand that. It helps to easily identify a worker. It serves a purpose. However, I have an SAT level problem with the discrimination allowed against tattoos and other forms of body art. Body modifications have absolutely nothing to do with a worker's performance, and vilifying them has everything to do with reinforcing stereotypes and appealing to prejudices.

It sounds a little something like this: "People with tattoos aren't smart. People with tattoos aren't professional. People with tattoos are criminals. People with tattoos are high school dropouts. Tattoos are nasty." Rinse. Repeat with body piercings.

In the majority of these cases, I think that this is completely stupid (much like the people who are making those statements). Sure, there are people in the world who dislike body art, and they probably wouldn't want someone who is "fashionably rebellious" to serve or work for them. Here is the thing though—they are *still* prejudiced toward an entire group of people. They are making judgments of others based on unproven, incorrect—or at least outdated—information. We cannot form a successful society based on the assumptions made by people who refuse to judge a person as an individual as opposed to a stereotype and expect to have a civil society. It doesn't work that way.

Appealing to their judgmental mindset is no longer an act of pleasing a customer; it is oppressing the workers. *Workers*, you know, goddamned human beings who can decide for themselves whether or not they want a design on their own body. In most cases, the creatively rebellious envision this art on their bodies long before it comes into existence, and they went through a decent amount of pain to make that vision a reality. What in the hell makes anyone think that an employer has a right to dictate what someone can or cannot place onto their own body? If that person is not your underaged kid, then you deserve **almost** no say in this matter.

Do you have any idea of how many things have been considered "undesirable" by customers? Let's run off a few stereotypes. Tattoos and body piercings are definitely at the top of the list, because obviously ink in the skin or metal in the face will prevent you from being able to learn any information. Therefore, you're automatically unable to perform a job outside of the artistic realm. Also, if you have those damned things, then you're *dirty*. Earrings are perfectly acceptable (if you're female), but if you take that *exact* same piece of metal and place it in your eyebrow, lip, or nose, then *clearly* you don't bathe.

Have you seen the looks that customers give cis women in the technology industry? That person was born with a vagina, so *clearly* she cannot handle any of your service needs; I mean, unless you need a sandwich or something else out of the kitchen. There is no possible way that a female and a male can have equal knowledge about this topic in present times, because everyone knows that women sleep their way into having everything that they possess.

People over the age of 50 are discriminated against as well. That person is "old," so obviously their knowledge is outdated. No way did that geezer go back to school, because school is for super young people only. You can't even get in past the age of 35. I think it's illegal or something. Besides, even if they had the knowledge, there is *no way* that they'd have the energy to perform a job that requires anything more than sitting in a plush chair making spit bubbles.

My personal favorite in the news lately is hair. No, I'm not referring to blue, pink, or purple hair, because everyone knows the dye's chemicals seep into the brain and cause violent tendencies. I'm talking about natural "African American" hair. You know, afros, cornrows, twist outs, dreadlocks—the hairstyles typically worn by African Americans with naturally curly hair. Those hairstyles are "dirty," "unprofessional"—and my new favorite adjective, "*distracting*." Yes, being born with wild, curly hair is definitely distracting. It's impossible to learn things with all of that crap blocking your brain. I mean, everyone knows that hair blocks you from processing thoughts, duh.

I know that some people would read this and say, "Well those things *are* unprofessional. Those people need to grow up and follow the rules. The world is not all peaches and cream, and they need to accept it."

To those people, I say, "I have a better idea." How about *you* grow up and realize that not everybody is going to look the way you do, or the way that *you* think *they* should look, and that's perfectly fine as long as they are able to perform the job that they set out to do? There are plenty of people who think that a stiff suit and tie makes a salesman look like a crook, should we ban those as well?

Oh, how about for the bonus round we briefly dip into the personal lives of a few groups? Women with kids? Yeah, they'll *never* come to work, better not hire those. However, hiring men with kids is fine. In fact, it is encouraged since they're the breadwinners who are just trying to provide for their families. It's such an upstanding and inspiring gesture. Who wouldn't hire them? They are *family men*. That other bitch is just trying to escape from the kitchen and her childrearing responsibilities.

Ex-convicts don't fair well either. In this country, we send people to prison so that they can be reformed from their life of crime, yet when they are released they'll be hard-pressed to find an employer who'll give them a chance to prove that they have been reformed. If no one will hire them, how are they supposed to survive? Without a job and without the ability to receive certain social programs, the only option is to— oh...right...turn to a life of crime. How ironic and *totally* not a problem!

These discrimination problems are just as real (and disgusting) for the creative minds around us. Companies often tout that they are in search of innovative thinkers, or those who can "think outside of the box." They also have to be *fresh* talent (because apparently people's minds expire after a certain age, and don't work anymore). Judging from what I've seen of my generation though, those creative, innovative people often spread that creativity to their bodies. It just doesn't stay contained to paper or the computer screen. However, one tattoo or piercing in the "wrong" place and companies will never look at that person twice. They want the artist's mind, not the artist as a whole.

It is time that we speak out against such practices. It should be frowned upon to practically attempt to factory farm thoughts and imagination in order to milk them from a person like a cow. Either they want the modified person and their thoughts, or they don't want anything. Humans are a packaged deal in that way. We are in the 21st century. I think that people should be able to decorate themselves without being discriminated against for being different.

People deserve to have the right to choose how they want to look, as long as that look does not present hatred toward another group. I mean, they can HAVE that tattoo, but no one should be forced to hire that person, because in that case it isn't just body art—it's a hate agenda. That *can* actually be harmful. That music note tattoo and blue hair isn't targeting anyone.

I once heard someone pose the question, "Why are tattoos considered to be so bad?" The other person replied, "It is unprofessional to have them because it is illegal to deface government property." I'm not 100% sure where I stand with that sentiment, but I do know that it is past time that we stop catering to other people's stereotypes. Perhaps if someone turns their nose up at a doctor or nurse for having a tattoo, then they don't deserve the skill that that person has to offer. I've worked retail, and the customer is not *always* right. Often times, the customer is an asshole, and someone needs to inform him or her of this.

I'm not sure if it's because I've had my own body art for so long, but I get extremely offended when other people sneer at the idea of tattoos and piercings. I could run off a list of my achievements and boast about how my record is squeaky clean, but I don't do that. Instead, I focus all of my energy on smiling and resisting the urge to say, "I look this way because I *choose* to look this way. It's my right to wear this body the way I see fit. I may look weird to you, but you look pathetic to me because of all the things that you could be in the world you chose to be an asshole. However, you still hold your job without a problem, so I don't see what the big deal is."

-X

Shopping (When You're Damn near Broke)

In just about every movie that I've seen, young adults were portrayed as carefree individuals who *love* to shop. They nearly leave their skeletons behind while speeding off inside a store every time they see a sale sign above a ridiculously priced, high-end item. Here is the thing though: in movies, they don't *actually* have to pay for anything. Most young adults do not have enough money for their bills, let alone for expensive clothing and electronic devices. Hell, cheap clothing is practically considered a luxury item when you're on a Ramen Noodle budget.

That being said, I am here to inform you that shopping when you're damn near broke is just no damn fun. You'll be hard-pressed to discover the amusement in being so broke that you start hoping that you can find a quarter, a nickel, and three pennies on the dressing room floor so you can be sure that you can cover the tax on this once in a lifetime chance purchase of a $3 clearance shirt. If you don't find this illusive currency, then you have one of two options:

1. You can buy the shirt on your debit card and pray that you don't overdraft (because of what I've told you about banks earlier). Let's be honest, you haven't achieved enough in life to have a company

offer you a credit card so that you can charge the items and eventually ruin your credit score, so that option is out. You're already bankrupt. You're ahead of the game!

2. The other option is that you can *leave the item there*. Sometimes you exercise this option with great shame, like when you've already started checking out before you remembered the bank's merry go 'round of fees and fuckery, and decided to leave the item at the counter in order to avoid that whole ordeal. The people behind you? Yes, that's judgment in their eyes. They are judging the ever-loving fecal matter out of you for your last minute wisdom. Your job is to ignore them (or flick them off if they get too harsh).

I suppose a third option would be to try to find someone to purchase the item for you, but unless it's a parent or another blood relative, then I wouldn't recommend it. Your friends would probably *love* to help you, but they probably scouring the dressing room floor for change harder than you did in hopes that you missed something.

In case you're one of the lucky ones whom this has never applied to (first of all, screw you, you probably judged me in line on ~~a few rare~~ several occasions), then keep reading. I've provided a list explaining why shopping sucks for people who are on a low budget, so that maybe you'll be less judgmental of the person in front of you who's seemingly playing tug of war with *every* item exchanged with the cashier.

WHY IT SUCKS TO SHOP WHEN YOU'RE (ALMOST) BROKE:

1. You have to watch other people shop without a care in the world while you're trying to find pennies that have been lost in your couch since second grade so that you can afford a $3 shirt.
2. Your card may get declined. Actually, despite the embarrassment, this is a blessing in disguise. I'm serious! If it had gone through, the bank would have made you pay a fee for overdrafting your checking account. The only problem is that it happens in front of other people. Upon witnessing your card's rejection, they *will* give you a look that screams, "Failure! You really should have had it together by now. What are you doing with your life? Your parents must be so ashamed."
3. If you had money to spend then nothing would be as appealing as it is now that you don't really have any money. If the item's appeal didn't change, then the size you need will only be available once you're broke. This happens far too often for it to be a coincidence.

4. Shopping online isn't fun either, because not only do you have to attempt to scrape money together for the tax, now you'll have to pay shipping costs. You couldn't cover 33 cents worth of tax, what in the hell makes you think that you can afford standard shipping? Besides, the typical $5.99 shipping rate is probably more expensive than the item that you were buying in the first place.

5. It forces you to remember how much money you *don't* have, and that's the first step of spiraling into a quarter life crisis—sometimes your second or third one, depending on how your year is going.

6. No two pieces of clothing are the exact same size, even when they are labeled as the same size. (This is due to human error.) This means that you have to try on each and every piece to see if it fits. Fun fact: Finding affordable clothing that you really need, and having it not fit is the reason there is a hell. That is a scientifically proven fact.

7. You have to see the mannequins wear clothing that you *desperately* need. It isn't even a real person for fuck's sake, and it can afford clothing that you cannot. You're struggling to find a way to look presentable to the world that you're trying to succeed in, and the items that you need belong to some fucker who doesn't even have any bones. That's so close to rock bottom you're practically snorting the pebbles.

8. You will begin to question where you went wrong with your life, but not in a productive way. It'll be more of a "woe is me" kind of way. You'll be inclined to drink your feelings away, but then you'll remember that you cannot afford the alcohol, if you're even old enough to buy it.

    Can you imagine wanting to go shopping now? I'm not sure where those people in the movies get their money from, but I have a feeling it is in the same place where they find all of those perfect spouses that don't exist in real life. They have done a fantastic job of hiding this place from me and most of the other young adults I know.

    In a time when there are people struggling to find work, I think it'd be healthier for us all if we let go of the idea that shopping is going to bring us something fulfilling. It won't. If you're depending on the amount of stuff that you have to tip the meter on the happiness scale, then you will be left disappointed, and let's face it, you've already experienced enough of that by caving into a brightly colored sign. There is no need to add an extra layer to the disappointment by trying to keep up with the Joneses when you're eight steps behind the Hillbillies.

    There's no way around it, being broke *sucks*. It is really frustrating to want or need something that you are unable to get for yourself. However, being broke also taught me that I don't *need* everything that I *want*, and the same is true for everyone else. Shopping and buying things will not bring true long term happiness, and likewise, it doesn't have to bring true long term sadness.

I'm not saying that we should be enthused to go without the things that we actually *need;* what I mean is that we can all use a healthy reality check about having everything that we *want*. Despite what we have been led to believe $5 coffees, $700 phones, 500 cable channels, $50 T-shirts, and the like are not necessary in order to have a happy life. We don't *need* these things; we're addicted to these things and the status that comes with them. It seriously skews our perception of the world and what other people have to live without—like clean water and food.

It is said that sometimes less is more. Well, I think that in this case sometimes none is even greater. If having those luxury items taken away from us is what it takes to make us more thoughtful people, then I welcome the process and all of its discomfort. Unlike college, not all lessons have to come with a huge price tag, which is great because most of us wouldn't be able to afford it otherwise.

-X

Clubs and Bars

If there is one thing that I am expected to do as a young adult, it is to frequently visit clubs and bars. I'm supposed to find some type of pleasure in getting excessively drunk—which I should have been doing since the moment I turned 16 anyway, and barely remembering it all the next day as I'm puking and nursing a headache. Hard partying has become synonymous with young adulthood. It is a rite of passage, if you will. However, putting someone like me in a club or a bar is like putting a cat in ice water. It is out of my element; I *will* avoid it at all costs, and if I find myself there I'm 127% sure that death is imminent.

It doesn't wait until you're 18 anymore, the pressure to party is starting earlier by the decade. There are an excess of teen clubs in my area, and the older teens just sneak into the 21 and over clubs anyway. I must admit, the overwhelming desire of my peers to be in these places made me extremely curious as to what a night out was really like, so I bit the bullet and went out one night.

I will never do that shit again.

Much like the other aspects of adult life, the projected image of going out versus what going out is *actually* like is about as similar as a koala bear and a peanut. It wasn't glamorous. It wasn't filled with exciting sights. It didn't enhance a worthy quality within anyone in the building. Most importantly, it didn't help my social abilities. In fact, I think it may have made them worse. I wish that I could have gotten on a loud speaker and informed every drunken individual in attendance of the following: You don't dance as well as you think you do. You're singing more off key than you think you are. You don't look anything like the people on television, and you damn sure don't need another drink. Stop. Just stop. You look like an asshole, and you smell funny. Go home.

However, it is inappropriate to say those things to people, so I didn't say anything. Instead, I observed the realities of night life as I solemnly swore that I'd never do that to myself again.

It started out innocently enough. A coworker was having a birthday celebration at a club, and I was invited. My first instinct was to turn down the invitation, but it isn't often that people are nice to the weird kid. In addition to the flattery, I was legitimately curious about this nightlife that everyone was raving on about, so I decided to accept the offer.

We began the night with an Italian dinner, and I was lured into a false sense of security because I started thinking that it wouldn't be so bad. I didn't know how quickly things could change until we reached the door of a bar. I'm not even sure I was old enough to get into this place, but my coworker was friends with the bouncer, so I was let in without question. I could not have been more than 25 feet inside of the building when I realized that I'd made a terrible mistake.

Do you want to know what going to a club is really like? Nightlife starts off with you walking into a room filled with a bunch of sweaty drunk people. The fact that the music is blasting at ear shattering levels makes them even more confident in their dancing skills. Actually, that was the first thing that I learned about going out. When you're in a club, your ability to dance is directly related to how loud the music is. It's like either you become convinced that the sound makes everyone around you blind, or the sound makes you forget that you can't dance. I'm not sure which it is.

As soon as you find a comfortable spot that you assume is out of every "dancer's" way, the drunk people start finding you. They want to know who you are and why you aren't dancing. They immediately want to dance with you. There are *hundreds* of other dancing drunks around, but they want *you*. You won't know whether to be flattered or repulsed, because it's like, *ALL OF* THE DRUNKEN DANCERS, AND YOU APPROACH THE ONLY SOBER PERSON? HOW DRUNK ARE YOU?

Alcohol destroys people's ability to realize that you don't want to talk to them. That was probably the worst part of it, the harassment. Hell, after a while even my coworkers became a harassment because they kept following me everywhere. They thought that I was attempting to be social with everyone in the club. Yes, the alcohol made them think that I was doing the exact opposite of what I was trying to do.

I take that back. The *worst* part had to have been the people who were so drunk that they found me attractive. I've learned that when you're in a club, if the music is loud enough, no one ASKS you to dance—they just start dancing with you. That was scary. That was absolutely terrifying, and I didn't like that shit one bit. I'd never had so many people (of both genders) rub their body parts against me without my permission. I'm sure that violated some sort of law, but I was in such a hurry to get the fuck out of that club that I didn't think about that aspect.

That's what clubs are typically like, but bars are different. See, at clubs everyone wants to dance and feel "sexy." In the process of trying to feel brave enough to dance badly in front of other humans, they just kind of end up drunk. However, at bars everyone goes there with the intention to drink until they puke. Actually, that's what bars remind me of—a watering hole. Everyone is impatient for their turn, they tend to show off their best assets, and somehow a fight always breaks out for no apparent reason. Literally, the only difference is that instead of drinking water the animals are drinking hard liquor—and yes, I said *ANIMALS*.

Bars are more expensive as well. I remember my coworker getting a $6 drink at the club, but the same one was $9 at the bar that we visited. That's another thing about going out, once your "friends" start partying they cannot seem to stop. You're not going to one club or bar; no, you're going to at least three. We ended up going to five that night. Do you know how *expensive* that is? It's no damn wonder young adults are so broke (like, even more than they should be). If my coworkers didn't know people, I would have easily spent at least $60 just getting into the places, that doesn't count drinks. Luckily, I don't drink.

Maybe I am totally alone in this feeling, but I think that clubs and the nightlife are highly overrated. I don't understand why anyone would pay to be harassed. I don't understand why anyone would pay $10 for a drink that costs $3 to make yourself. I don't understand why I'd go to a place to be around people who I'm too uncomfortable with to dance in front of while sober. I don't understand any of it.

This may be the one thing that people will claim is a direct result of my social anxiety issues. The truth is, if that's the case, then I don't mind. I'd rather be socially anxious and find a few people who make me *so* comfortable that I don't need to be drunk to be stupid around them than to be "normal" and not realize that

I'm paying to impress people whom I'm afraid of. I've said it a million times, masking a problem will *never* make it go away; it only makes it bigger when we have to deal with it. However, impressing people in this scene is something that I no longer have to deal with because I walked away from the problem myself, and I don't intend to go back.

-X

Things That Don't Make Sense to Me

There was a time when I thought I had a lot of life figured out, and it turns out that I didn't know anything. However, there was also a time when I thought I didn't know anything about life, but when the time came and I needed something, I figured it out. I knew more than I thought I did, and that was a lovely surprise. However, there are still quite a few things about life that I know for a fact that I have not figured out yet, and I'd like to share some of those with you.

The first one is quite arbitrary, but it bothers me. Why on Earth did my desk get smaller the longer I stayed in school? In Pre-K, we were seated on the floor. We had an *entire floor* as our desk. How freeing is that? In Kindergarten, we were seated together at long tables. In grades one through five, my desk was a miniature table, and very individual. When I got to middle school, I basically had a hovering lunch tray as a desk, and by the time I got to high school the hovering lunch tray must have been half eaten, because it was a lot smaller.

I don't know if schools have noticed this, but we get bigger as we grow up—switch the damn desks around. It isn't like we have eons of extra people in high school who weren't there in middle school (at least in my area) to be able to justify a need for smaller desks in order to save space. The more room we need the less we're given. I fail to understand this in every way.

Maybe I don't understand other people in general, but I look at the shopping habits of other people and find myself so confused. I cannot believe that I live in a place where people will pay $5 for a single, tall cup of coffee, but those *same* people will complain that a gallon of milk is $4. That cup of coffee is approximately 12 ounces. The gallon of milk is 128 ounces. You can literally pour about ten and a half of those $5 coffees into this one $4 gallon of milk, and yet the price of milk is what is considered outrageous. Okay, sounds legit.

Now I don't wear this stuff, so I admittedly have no place talking about it. However, outside looking in, I do not understand why putting on mascara or eyeliner requires a person's mouth to be open. I've purposefully observed many females (and a few males) putting on these eye essentials, and every single one of them had to open their mouths to apply it decently. I don't even know where to begin on how much I don't understand that. Seriously! If I want to make my lashes longer, then I need to part the Red Sea in order to comb through them?

What really amazes me is that there seems to be a direct relationship of how experienced a person is with cosmetics, and how widely they open their mouth while applying these products. I'm pretty sure most "experts" only slightly part their lips. The intermediate users may have enough room for a fly to circle in and out a couple of times. A beginner, though? Oh my God, a beginner can usually fit a basketball into their mouth while putting on mascara. If you really want a show, try watching people attempt to put this shit on their eyes. You'll be completely confused about the purpose of makeup. It's supposed to make them prettier, but here it is causing lockjaw, and making healthy people everywhere look like they are having a stroke.

There's always the issue of love and other emotional tragedies. I know that this question has been asked approximately 18 kajillion times, but *seriously:* WHY DO WE DEVELOP CRUSHES ON PEOPLE WHO DO NOT LIKE US BACK? I know that the go-to reasoning is that getting our hearts broken and our egos bruised will help us to build character, strength, and emotional maturity, but has anyone ever bothered to verify this? Has anyone ever proven that developing feelings that cause us to have heart palpitations, release various bodily fluids, and harbor a load of flying insects in our stomachs—only to have the person we feel them for reject us—do *anything* positive for us? I think it's bullshit!

The only thing that has happened to my character is that it probably became emotionally unstable, and questioned whether or not it even belonged in the plot that it found itself inside. You haven't truly been rejected by someone until they make you feel like if your life were a story, you wouldn't even be the main character. I'm not sure if I've built any strength emotionally, but orally my language has become a lot stronger over the past few years. As for emotional maturity, if that means becoming sick of the same *old* shit day after day, then pass me the prunes because I'm ready to drop this load. I'm emotionally qualified for my AARP card and Life Alert gift package. I am THAT mature.

Do you know what else doesn't make sense to me about people? Well, this applies to females only, but how is it that a chick has the ability to grow an entire human body within her body, but if she loses an arm then she's just ass-out of a fucking arm? You mean to tell me her body can grow an entirely different brain, heart, trunk, and all of this other shit, but it can't regrow itself another limb?

If you don't agree with the viewpoint of the female growing the baby, and you feel as though the baby grows itself, then that makes it even worse. Now you're telling me that we can grow ourselves when we don't even have a fully developed brain, but once we do, then we can't grow any more things? Doesn't this seem backwards to anyone else? I feel like we should be able to grow even more body parts with a fully developed brain. We can all use an extra hand at times. This should definitely be a thing.

I'm not sure why this surprises me though, because our brains also do this thing where they scare the shit out of themselves. Yeah, those things are called nightmares, and they're another item on the list of things that I just *cannot* comprehend. I know that dreams are not well understood, but I cannot deal with the fact that our brains are *so* damn psychotic that they'll disregard their need for sleep in order to create scenarios that never really happened, mentally put us inside these situations, and literally scare us into consciousness. Our brains want us to feel fear so badly that causing us to jump to conclusions, making us afraid to speak in front of other humans, and other forms of non-useful "protection" are not enough. No, if it cannot make us afraid of real things, then it'll just make some shit up to show us while we're trying to honor its sleep requirement.

The brain doesn't stop with its confusing ways regarding sleep there, because it doesn't do *anything* half-assed. Let's think about this logic: I am sleepy. I have a couple more things to do before I can take a nap, perhaps feed the cat or finish up some homework. I do those things, then I lay down to go to sleep. Suddenly I have the energy to run ten marathons, paint a couple of houses, rebuild a few car engines, and then have breakfast.

Why? Why do our bodies do this? It's overcompensation to the highest degree. It isn't just high energy though; we're literally a little bit crazy when we're having this experience—or at least I am. Everything becomes extremely funny when I'm in this state of mind. You don't know true exhaustion until you're sitting on the floor, in tears, laughing at the fact that cats don't have any cheeks.

Society has its fair share of things that I don't understand either. Employment issues absolutely top the list in this area, and it isn't just because I do not in any way, shape, or form, understand how to operate a fax machine. There is the issue with the job schedule itself. Why is it that we have to work until certain times? Like, if we're finished with our work at 2:00 p.m., then why in the world do we have to stay until 5:00 p.m. just to get paid the same amount of money? We still did the same amount of work; it just didn't take us as long because we're awesome. We have to be punished for our time efficiency now? Obviously this doesn't apply to jobs like food service, retail, and medical positions, but I'm talking about the typical office job. It is supposed to be work, not a jail sentence. This is why people spend most of their workday playing on the Internet.

Speaking of the Internet, why the hell are jobs so obsessed with what people post on social media? I mean, it's nice to have a general idea of the type person someone is, but the fact that people can get fired for a drunken picture doesn't make any sense if you really think about it. First of all, being drunk isn't exactly illegal. (There's the issue of public intoxication, but that isn't necessarily the case in a picture. That person could be drunk at home, or at a friend's home.) Second of all, if a person is not drunk while on the job, or if the drunkenness is not affecting their ability to do their job, then their boss has no business worrying about their consumption level. Their liver and loved ones should handle that (within reason).

Dear future bosses, an employee's private life is none of your business. You are not their parent. You should go be the boss and demand some coffee or something. You can't just stalk employees' social media profiles. Like, if you can stalk their profiles, then they should be able to call it unprofessional fraternizing, because that is crush-like behavior.

After being out in the "real world" for about five seconds, I have learned that we really need good credit in order to make life a bit easier. Do you want to know what we need in order to establish good credit? Good credit! What the fudge cake, holy crap, somebody help me because I do not compute. A personal example of this is when I needed to buy a new mattress. My parents decided that I needed to start building my credit, so the purchase was going to be in my name. (I was working at the time.) We were all surprised when I could not get a line of credit despite my income, savings, and down payment—simply because I had not previously had credit. How in the world are we supposed to build credit by having credit to begin with? Where does this initial credit come from? The credit fairy? That bitch has not paid me a visit, and I'm pretty sure that she's planning on standing me up for at least another 20 years.

Finally, this has to be the thing that confuses me the most: the double standards regarding young adult life between males and females. Actually, it's a very specific thing. As young adults, we are encouraged to try to experience as much as we can while we "have the chance." We are led to believe that the young adult years should be spent traveling, partying, and having lots of life-complicating sex. However, it seems that only one gender is allowed the freedom to participate in the last challenge, and it is not the females.

Now don't get me wrong, I'm not saying that everyone should sleep with everyone, or that everyone should wait until marriage (or anything in between). What I'm saying is that I don't understand how society would encourage sleeping around for one gender and not the other one, but also demonize same-sex couples. If girls cannot participate in the activities without being "whores," and if sleeping with someone of the same sex is "wrong"—then who the hell are these young boys supposed to sleep with? There's no one left. Is this supposed to be a clever way to tell everyone to masturbate? I see no other solution to this equation that society has created.

I'm pretty sure there are plenty of other things that I still don't understand, some of which are probably much more complicated than the few that I mentioned, but these are definitely at the very top of the list. It seems as though everyone tries to pretend that they know everything, and that's another thing that I don't understand. There are billions upon billions of things and thoughts in this world. There is no way that any one person will ever know what all of them mean or how to deal with them.

We can never understand *everything*, if we did, then we'd lose our sense of imagination and wonder. What we need to do is get comfortable admitting that there are things that are just out of our brain's computing ability. There will be things in life, both silly and serious, that we just don't understand, but knowing that we'll never know *everything* is really the only thing that we ever truly need to understand.

-X

RELATIONSHIPS

Best Friends

There's nothing like a best friend, is there? That one person in your life who makes you feel like your parents must be secretly wanted in five states for kidnapping you from another couple, because there is no *way* that your "BFF" is not your brother or sister. You share countless inside jokes that make you both laugh until your sides feel like a shirt that's way too damn tight. There is nothing in the world that you can't tell your best friend without the fear of judgment. You know your secrets are safe. You know that your presence is wanted. If given the chance, you'd never live more than a short drive away from each other. Here is the problem: As you two become professional adults, the relationship may change…if it even still exists.

Yes, you read that correctly. One day your best friend may not actually be your best friend anymore. I know you think that it is completely impossible for this to happen. I know you're retorting, "Ha! That wouldn't happen with me and *my* BFF. We're thicker than a bowl of brownie batter with extra walnuts." You know, I really hope that you're right. However, the harsh truth is that if you *are* right, then you're the exception. I'm lucky enough to have one exception who is currently in my life, but I'm experienced enough to have five friends who were not an exception. Do you remember the group of coworkers whom I went to the club with? Well, this is the lesson that knowing them for two years beyond that night taught me.

A vague "something" happens after you've known someone for a long time. You start to notice little annoyances that you swear were not there before, and your ability to remain polite when you're not in a good mood begins to decline. The time you spend together is no longer carefree. You don't look forward to talking with this person. Your friend is becoming increasingly annoying as your life changes, and you aren't really sure why. Sometimes you won't feel the growing annoyance, but your friend will feel like this toward you. You'll start to notice that you're being treated differently, and you can't figure out what the hell is going on.

The signs that you're about to have a vacancy in the spot of your heart where your best friend goes are *ridiculously* obvious in retrospect, so I'm going to tell you some of them in the hopes that you can brace yourself for the fallout. These apply to both guys and girls, but for writing purposes I'm just going to use the pronoun "her" since most of my coworkers were female.

SIGNS YOU'RE ABOUT TO GET KICKED OUT OF THE FRIEND ZONE:

1. **Texts are no longer funny.** The little skank may not even answer you back. This is the most obvious sign, but we tend to make excuses for it. We may blame the phone service, or your friend may SWEAR that she texted you back, and that you somehow didn't receive the message. Either way, the constant texting is no longer fun. You may even neglect her texts to spend time with your family. That's when you know shit is seriously going downhill.

2. **When you trip and fall in public, she asks if you're okay before she laughs.** Your best friend will laugh at you first and tend to your pride later because she knows that you love her. Let's face it, even if you do get mad, you'll just forgive her 25 seconds later anyway. Do you know who wouldn't feel comfortable laughing at your misfortune directly in your face? A stranger. Your best friend is becoming a stranger.

3. **You start getting back the items that you lent her.** In other words, she doesn't want you around. She doesn't even want *your stuff* around. Think about it, when was the last time you EVER got an item back from her? Best friends keep your stuff. That's why you're always at each other's house, you're visiting your items.

4. She **asks for something from your refrigerator.** She asks. When you're best friends, your house *IS* her house. You don't *ask* for each other's food—you just *take* it. Get that weird creature standing in your kitchen away from you, but first find out what it did with your best friend. (It probably ate her.)
5. **You become responsible for the bulk of the conversation.** Unless you have an introverted best friend, then you two probably talk all over each other's sentences due to the sheer excitement of the conversation. Often times, neither one of you can get a word in edgewise, let alone do either of you have to fight to find something to say to each other, which brings me to my next point…
6. **Silences become awkward.** You're not truly best friends unless you're so comfortable while hanging out with her that sometimes you forget that she's there. The only reason that you remember is that she says something, and you have a quick mental debate with yourself as to whether or not you're insane. It'll scare the crap out of you, and she will laugh. You won't even feel embarrassed let alone awkward. Awkward silences are for new friends, ex-lovers, and strangers.
7. **She calls your mom and dad by their real names.** My late friend always called my mom and dad, well, Mom and Dad. I called his mom and dad—you guessed it, Mom and Dad. If a friendship is at

the point where you two start using the whole "Mrs. ____ & Mr. ____" thing to address each other's parents, then it's practically already over.

8. **She doesn't warn you when she'll be absent from school or work (if those things apply).** She *abandoned* you. You were fucking *abandoned*. Everyone knows that you only play hooky when your best friend isn't going to be at work or school (unless you're covering for her, or you're practically dying). Why? Because if she was sick, then you'd go to take care of her. No one else is allowed to see her plummet from a perfect 10 to a solid 2 and a half except you. If she wasn't sick, then you'd be playing hooky together. In fact, you two would probably end up doing something so crazy that you'd both have to miss work or school the next day as well, except for legitimate reasons. You'd need to recover from your day off. However, you weren't informed, and that's a terrible sign. I'm so sorry, consider this a hug.

Chances are you'll know in your gut when something just doesn't click the way that it used to. Denying these things never make it better, but the important thing to remember is that no one is to blame for this. A hard truth of growing up is that some best friends will grow apart. The lives that we live mimic the planet that we live on. Our entire existence is a continuous state of cycles and seasons. The people whom we meet throughout our time on this planet are like leaves to a tree. Their presence and the beauty that they bring help us to blossom into something breathtakingly stunning. We wouldn't be who we are if they weren't a part of us.

However, at some point, leaves begin to change color due to no fault of their own. Their lives are cycling against their will just like ours. The process may render something beautiful to everyone else, but for us, we're faced with the fact that our leaves are dying. Their time with us is over, and we have to let them go so that we can survive. We weren't born to be evergreens. Our beauty lies within the way we constantly return from our barren state with new life, and a greater appreciation for the leaves that we get to hold onto.

A relationship does not have to stay exactly the same for it to be valuable. It doesn't have to be "the end" because things change. It just has to be different, and different isn't always bad. In fact, sometimes it can be even better. I mean, having so much love for another human being that it allows you to accept the fact that you're also a leaf to *her* tree is a beautiful thing. Letting someone move on without animosity can be difficult, but I can't think of a better gift from a true best friend.

-X

Life Lesson #3
The Reality of Crushes

What you hope your crush thinks of you

What your crush actually thinks of you*

*If they notice you

Crushes

Sweaty palms, racing thoughts, shaky limbs, pounding heart, and unexplained insects flying around aimlessly in your stomach—there's nothing in the world quite like having a crush, is there? In the matter of a few days (or maybe just a few minutes) another human being comes along and completely flips your world upside down, leaving you with approximately 7% of your original sanity on a good day.

You start doing weird things like smiling to yourself when you think about that person (creeper). Then there's the infamous symptom of writing their name all over your stuff, or imagining scenarios in which they confess their undying love for you. Don't even get me started on that goofy expression that takes over your face when you're texting each other (if you've gotten to the point where you've mustered up your confidence to get their number, that is). Oh, that look is the *worst*. It looks like a combination of needing to sneeze, and trying to expel an exceptionally large turd. There is no human alive who can successfully pull off this expression, but you don't mind looking stupid, because you *feel* AWESOME.

At some point, you will begin to imagine marriage, buying a home, taking lavish vacations together, and what your kids would look like, but that usually happens only after you've been legitimately crushing for approximately three to five days. What I'm trying to say is that it makes you *batshit crazy*.

We've all been there at one point, some of us more than others. I've only had the pleasure of having a legitimate, "Holy fuck, I think I'm losing my mind, someone please have me committed—but have me committed in a place where I can still *see* that Demigod or I'll *die*" type of crush once in my life. However, that experience was enough for me. Actually, I'd be willing to say that it was *more* than enough. I cannot handle another one of those things. I hope my brain has disabled that feature in its settings. I have had one other minor crush on someone, and while that type of crush can be a little scary they are *much* less entertaining, so we're going to talk about the other kind. (And I'm going to do so using "their" as a singular pronoun because I'm an anonymous rebel blogger with a cause!)

As I've said, for some crushes it's no big deal. You'll see someone and think, "Oh, look at that human. That one is really cute." Then you'll slowly develop a fondness toward that person. On the *other* hand, there are times when you'll see someone and your common sense panics and makes a break for the nearest window. Do you know that tingly feeling that you get when you see your crush? That's all of the common sense leaving your body at an alarming rate. There are an infinite amount of stupid things that you'll do when you like someone, but I'll just fill you in on the basics so that you can hopefully do some damage control.

First, you'll start to imagine yourself in a relationship with this person before you actually talk to them to find out if you remotely like their personality. This is the move that will get you into the most trouble, because it provides ample opportunity to get your hopes up to unfulfillable amounts. (I'm not even sure if unfulfillable is a word, but if it isn't, know that it is still more realistic than the fantasies that you've created.) You'll start to imagine all of these scenarios that you'll laugh at in the beginning, but then at some point, you'll start to believe that they'll eventually happen. You'll start waiting for it to happen, and then it won't happen —*then* you'll be disappointed because this other human didn't follow along with your imagination. #SignsThatYoureCrazy.

If you've reached the point in your crushlationship where you've actually spoken to this person, then the stupid things that you do will begin to compile on top of the first stupid thing. It's like a tiered cake of stupidity. For example, you'll have a conversation with this person and totally read everything that they are doing as flirting, because in your mind, this person is already yours. You're looking for things to prove your point instead of looking at the picture as a whole. In reality, they're probably just being polite instead of flirting. This isn't necessarily a bad thing though, because at least it shows that you've crushed on a person who is polite. That's actually a good thing! Just wait until you've crushed on an asshole, then you'll understand what I mean.

Text messages are probably your main source of inspiration when it comes to your imagination creating scenarios that are hell-bent on ruining your life. There is not only the possibility that you may honestly misread a text (and reply accordingly), but there is also the possibility that you will read it in the voice that you want to hear them use. You may read it to suit you and your feelings, which only makes it harder for you to be logical. There is a positive side to this though, and it's that you'll probably start looking on the bright side of *everything*, despite the situation at hand. Your train of thought may sound something like, "Oh? My parents are losing the house? That's okay. I can live in the Demigod's tree. I'll keep burglars from getting inside unnoticed. I've always wanted to be closer to nature anyway."

Seriously, your thoughts take an *extreme* shift into the realm of positivity when you have a crush, because your brain is hopped up on dopamine, oxytocin, and other "feel good" hormones that make you want to cuddle and shit like that. You're not imagining that part. You really are high to Jupiter on the presence of another human being. It doesn't seem like there is anything in the world that can break you, because you found the superhero you need in that other person (or so you hope).

Did you think the insanity would stop there? It won't. You haven't started to feel jealous over someone you aren't actually dating. Oh, you have? Then welcome to level two of the crazy things you do when you have an intense crush. At this point your hopes are up so high, that you cannot tolerate the thought of them being obliterated by disappointment. You have convinced yourself that it is only a matter of time before you two are an official couple. Needless to say, when you see your crush with someone else you become jealous. The part that sucks the most is that you cannot say anything about it, because honestly, how does this sound?

"Hey, I just wanted to let you know that I'm confronting you about how much you've been hanging out with [insert other person's name here]. I don't like it. I feel like you and I should be spending more time together. After all, you're mine. I know we aren't dating or anything, but I've claimed you already. You can't talk to that other person because it hurts my ego."

That sounds absolutely batshit crazy! So yes, you may *feel* jealousy burning every inch of your skin, but you cannot *say* that, because you have no right to order this other human to comply with the shit that you've created in your own fantasies.

This jealousy tends to lead you to do the next stupid thing, which is to hate the person your crush is interested in. Actually, you hate the person that your crush *seems* to be interested in. You've been creating scenarios of this person in your head for weeks, and it is highly likely that you are imagining his or her interest in this other person as well. After all, you did name your kids after being in the general vicinity of your crush for about three days, so I'd take what you think with a grain of salt.

Your friends are of no use to you either. They are so excited for you that they'll often misread the "signs" just as badly as you do. You all feed off of each other's nonsense—that's why you're friends. In fact, your friends may insult the person your crush is hanging out with, this "threat," even more quickly than you do. The crush insanity is contagious. You all need help at this point.

However, as much as you love your friends, if your crush asks you to hang out at *any* given time, then you will have an urge to ditch the CRAP out of them. It'll get to the point where you're almost pissed off that you even know your friends, because now your (over) confidence is showing, and your pals here are just being stage five cockblockers. Chances are they'll forgive you, or have even done it to you before, but try not to burn all of your bridges for this person, okay? You'll need someone to obsessively text the next time your crush "may have winked, but it may have been a blink."

Sometimes you let your crush fester for months before you even speak to the object of your affection, and sometimes when you *finally* speak to them, you learn that you have absolutely *nothing* in common. However, because you've been fantasizing for months about how perfect this person has to be, you decide you have to remedy this by FINDING something you two can fall in love over. Once you've realized that you cannot change that person, then you may try to change yourself. I cannot tell you how strongly I do not recommend this, because you'll never be able to keep the act up long term.

It doesn't even have to be anything super drastic, in fact, you may not initially notice that you're doing it. However, one day you'll probably find yourself trying to be interested in the same things that your crush is interested in. You want to impress them, so even though you find their hobby about as entertaining as cutting the entire lawn with a nail clipper, you continuously submerge yourself into this activity in the hopes that it'll make your crush want you (or just notice you). The problem is that even if you succeed—rather, *especially* if you succeed—then you've done a great job of false advertising. You are not the person that you presented to your crush, and now you'll be stuck acting like your false self as long as you want to keep them. You could have avoided this, you know, but you were busy imagining shit for three months before you said, "Hello."

No modern crush is complete unless you've done something as innocently creepy as stalking their social media profiles. This is an area where you had better tread carefully because there is so much potential for this to go drastically wrong, and make you seem like so much more of a creeper than you *actually* are (as hard as that may be to believe). Have you ever accidentally double tapped someone's Instagram picture from about two years ago? Yeah, try to explain that one to them, especially when you may not be friends with them on this social network.

I know what some of you are thinking, and it goes a little something like, "Well, I'll just make an anonymous profile to prevent accidents like that." Yeah, because making an entirely separate profile with a fake name to secretly (but safely) look at someone else's social media profile is *totally* normal, and not in any way creepy. That is 120% stalker behavior, but I've known otherwise sane people who have done it.

Some of the other crazy things that we do are far more lighthearted. For example, have you ever put cute emoji's by your crush's contact information in your phone? Have you ever found yourself smiling to yourself when you're thinking about that person? Admit it, you've got at least one item with his or her name scribbled on it. You've listened to their playlists to see what kind of music they're interested in. Those are *adorable* little actions. I'm not sure what adjective to use to describe the things I mentioned earlier in this post, but rest assured that you are not the only human being to have experienced such inner chaos.

The problem with crushes is that they are often one-sided. As hard as it may be for you to imagine while you're in the throes of infatuation, chances are this person doesn't remotely like you back. That's why it's called a crush. You're about to have your hopes, dreams, heart, and ego *crushed* by the weight of rejection. You know what though? It's okay. It's okay, because while most of what you did could be classified as borderline (or official) insanity, at least you experienced a level of excitement that you probably wouldn't have felt otherwise. Crushes make life ~~stressful~~ exciting, and if you can keep in mind that this person doesn't owe you anything, then you'll probably recover soon.

However, it seems as though lately we've somehow started thinking that people are "supposed" to like us back, or that our crush is somehow responsible for our feelings. They aren't. Your crush has absolutely *no* obligation to like you back. You have an obligation not to make a fantasy so damn intense that you start to believe it yourself. Unless this person explicitly told you that they had romantic feelings for you when they knew that they didn't, then they didn't lead you on. You led yourself on. You created much of your own disappointment. You cannot be angry at another person because they didn't share the same feelings that you did. They cannot *make* themselves like you in the same way that you couldn't make yourself *not* like them. Sometimes you like people who don't like you back—that's just another sucky part of life.

Sure, you probably did some really stupid things at the height of your crush, but you shouldn't really be ashamed that you did them. As long as you didn't harm anyone, other than your ego, then it's okay. I've recently learned that egos *are* meant to get bruised sometimes. It's like exercise for the emotions. It'll burn, hurt, and be extremely sore for some time afterward, but the result is a pretty impressive strength gain. You'll learn to live without a person whom you were convinced that you couldn't have a future without, and while it doesn't mean that no one can ever hurt you again, hopefully it gives you a little comfort in knowing that you *can* survive intense emotional disappointment.

The good news is that you were probably looking at this person through a giant pair of rose colored glasses anyway. I'm sure your crush is a great person, but no where near as great as you made them out to be. As impossible as it may seem now, you're going to meet someone who will make you really happy that it didn't work out with your crush. That person will come along, and make you completely *lose your shit* in a way that you have never done in the past. That's totally understandable, because this new interest is literally the best person *ever,* the next one always is.

-X

.

Nothing Conversations

When you become a young adult, you may realize that you are expected to do things that don't make any sense. One of those things is to have, what I like to call, a "nothing conversation." If you were born in the '90s or before, then you may remember this television show called *Seinfeld*. Its tagline stated that it was a show about nothing. It portrayed a group of friends living out an average day to day life, but the actual show never had a set theme. A nothing conversation is like that, but multiplied by approximately a billion. It is by far the most pointless thing that I've ever experienced, and it isn't nearly as entertaining as *Seinfeld*.

This isn't to be confused with small talk, which is when you politely tell a stranger hello and ask how he or she is doing. That is acceptable. A nothing conversation is when you talk to someone who, for whatever reason, you don't particularly want to talk to. However, due to social convention, you just kind of *have* to talk to them. This leads to not wanting the conversation to get too personal, and therefore you'll be careful of about you say. By the end of the conversation, neither of you will have said anything with any definite purpose, and you'll both be glad that the act is over. I'll give you a short example of a nothing conversation:

Unwilling Participant 1: "Hi! How are you?"

Unwilling Participant 2: "Oh you know how things go. What about you?"

Unwilling Participant 1: "What can I say, you know? It is what it is."

Unwilling Participant 2: "Yes. Yes, indeed."

Unwilling Participant 1: "I don't know what the world is coming to. Crazy stuff going on though, yeah?"

Unwilling Participant 2: "Oh yeah, things aren't like they used to be."

Unwilling Participant 1: "No, but we just have to keep going."

Unwilling Participant 2: "That's right, you can't quit."

Unwilling Participant 1: "No, you can't."

Unwilling Participant 1: "Well let me let you get going."

Unwilling Participant 2: "Yeah, I'll see you around."

What the hell did this conversation accomplish? The sad part is that this can go on for 20 or 30 minutes at a time—sometimes longer! I frequently hear my parents have conversations like this with their old classmates. I don't even know why they still enjoy casually running into someone at the grocery store, which is always where these conversations seem to take place. If I had to experience this every time I saw an old classmate, I'd probably move to a different state just to avoid the awkwardness that these conversations spawn.

It's like we've become so pressured to talk to people that we'll do anything to maintain our politeness, as defined by society, rather than just making things easier on ourselves and others by not talking to people with whom we don't want to share anything. However, since it *is* your job as an adult to uphold an image, I'm going to tell you how to survive the awkward nature of a nothing conversation. After all, social anxiety has given me lots of practice.

The first line of defense against a nothing conversation is to try to avoid any of the people in question. Just as you do while driving, make sure to constantly scan the surrounding area very quickly. If you should see anyone who would cause you to have an awkward, nothing conversation, then immediately go the other way. I don't care what you need in the store. I don't care if you're going to the emergency room because you're bleeding profusely from the nipples. It can wait until the coast is clear, because nothing will hurt you more than that conversation you're about to participate in.

If your scanning skills are not yet at the professional level, then there is a chance that instead of avoiding this person, you will accidentally make direct eye contact with them. Other times, the person will see you before you see them. First of all, please work on this. It'll make your life so much easier if you just know how to run away. Second, and most importantly, not all hope is lost at this point. I know. I really am *that* good.

The bad news is that unless you want to be completely rude, then you must acknowledge this person in some way. The good news is that you may be able to keep the verbal exchange to an absolute minimum, and by minimum I mean zero to fifteen words. How can you accomplish such a feat? You will pretend that you are in the world's *biggest* rush, and you will either nod or wave with a friendly smile, and speed off into any direction in which they were not headed—except backwards. If you turn around, that person will know you're avoiding them. For added effect, you may want to add in, "Hey! Do you know where [name an item] is? I'm in a rush." If you really want to make sure you don't come off as a prick, then as you're speeding by add, "Wow, you're looking great!" However, don't you dare stop walking, not even long enough to hear the thank you that may follow. I mean, if you go ahead and compliment a balding (or bald) person on their hair, then I highly doubt that a thank you is what you'll be receiving, but it doesn't matter, because you won't be there!

If the person insists on talking to you, even after you've proclaimed that you were in a rush, then your next move is to respond with short, dry answers as you keep walking. I'm serious. I know it sounds rude (because it IS), but if you don't care to talk to the person in the first place, then do you *really* care about what they think of your behavior? This person is acting like a four-year-old who is constantly nagging for attention when its mother is doing something of extreme importance, so treat them like one.

Now, if you're on the bus or some other public place where you cannot escape, then I hope you have a cell phone, because if you do, you're about to have the best conversation in the world with an imaginary person. If you're able to call an actual person, then you should do so. That will be better. However, if you cannot, then just be sure to put your phone on silent. You wouldn't want to be in the middle of a "conversation" only to have the phone ring into your ear. If this does happen, then you can just pretend that the call was dropped without you noticing it. However, it is much better to avoid that situation altogether.

Now, if you're stuck in a public place where you don't want to disturb others (or call attention to yourself) with your conversation—real or otherwise—then I hope that you have an iPod or something. I cannot express to you the thanks I must give my headphones on the weekly basis. Sure, I may be deaf toward the end of my life, but that may be a blessing in disguise. I mean, at least I won't have to be faced with the threat of an awkward conversation. People are complaining about having to press one for English when calling technical support, so I don't think that anyone who isn't constantly in my life would bother to learn sign language just to annoy me with awkward conversations.

If all else fails, then you may have an actual stalker, because believe it or not, most people can tell when conversation is unwanted. (This doesn't apply to social disorders, in which case, stop being an asshole.) However, you officially aren't allowed to fully blame this person, because you haven't done the one thing that properly gets your point across. See, when I was a child, I was often told that lying was a bad thing—and it is—however, "Not saying the truth" is almost just as bad. I personally think that the adult thing to do would be to say hello and explain that you either cannot or do not want to have a conversation. It doesn't even have to be all that rude, you can simply say, "Hi! Sorry I can't stop and talk, but it was nice to see you!" Let's be honest though, you aren't going to do that, and neither will I, because we're too damn scared of the judgment that we'd receive. It would be so much simpler logically, but so much harder socially that we would rather endure unnecessary stress in order to avoid discomfort, and that doesn't make you rude. That just makes you human.

-X

Dating

I'll be the first to admit that I've never been good at communicating with other people. I'm baffled by the rules of social interaction at the most basic level, but I *seriously* do not understand this whole dating thing that my generation has altered beyond the point of anything that was once recognizable to the human brain. I don't think anyone understands the dating game anymore, not even the people who are actively playing it, and that's because it doesn't make any fucking sense.

First of all, the steps of the damned thing are impractical because if you want to go on a date with someone whom you don't see often, then you have to make your intentions known right at the beginning—*sort of*—or you risk being thrown into the emotional hell known as the friend zone. However, at the same time you're not supposed to come off as being too desperate for a date.

The process is supposed to be something like this:

> 1. Locate a person who you'd be interested in dating.

> 2. Approach him or her without coming off as a creeper.

3. Talk to this person without telling them that you're interested in a date, because that's "creepy" to reveal within two minutes of meeting someone, and you don't want to seem desperate.

4. Hang out with them so that you get to know them, but don't tell them what you're *really* thinking about them yet.

5. Wait some unspecified amount of time, then reveal the truth.

6. Ask this person on a date.

7. Go on a date*

8. Bad Date = Never talk to the person again
   Good Date = Immediately become a couple

9. Wait for some unspecified amount of time again.

10. Break up or get married

*Note that step number seven is dependent upon the feelings   of another person. There's a possibility that you will be turned down. If rejection occurs, please visit "The Friend Zone" post for further instruction.

Can we talk about what is wrong with this? There is *so* much wrong with this. The first step seems relatively normal, except now that online dating is a thing, you may not even be looking at the person whom you are "interested" in. There is an entire television show dedicated to this shit, so this one only makes sense if things are happening "IRL." It may be hard to come off as normal in real life, but it seems damn near impossible not to sound "pervy" when you're asking a person, whom you haven't even met yet, for a date via an Internet profile.

To be honest, even in real life, I never really knew why I wanted to talk to the people whom I was interested in anyway. I didn't know anything about them when I decided that I "liked" them. The truth is that when I saw them my insides started tingling. That is the entire explanation. For all I know, that shit could mean that they are poisonous. After all, no one else I love comes with the side effect of making me feel like I have arthritis cream slathered all over my vital organs. That alone should tell me that crushes and dating are two things that I should avoid, but *no, I* generally take it as a sign that I should campaign for that person's affection.

What do you even say to someone when you're in this situation? "Hi, I saw you while you weren't looking at me—I'm totally not a creeper—*anyway*, when I saw you I started to tingle a little bit. I like tingling. Would you like to meet me some place at a later date so that you can make me tingle some more?"

No! It isn't socially acceptable to say that, so what do you do? YOU *LIE*. You have to lie about the tingles and the fact that you have them. Instead, you feel obligated to walk up to them and start a conversation about everything except what you're actually thinking about, which is really just a fancy version of a lie. That's right, before you start a relationship or have a disagreement, you're already lying to the object of your (often misplaced) affection.

The second step seems okay at first glance. I mean, sure, it will probably involve checking your appearance 10,000 times, and there will be awkward pauses, but at least it is simple, right? Wrong. *Fortunately*, society has become more accepting of different sexual orientations, so different types of dating are more common now. You don't really know if the person whom you possibly want to go on a date with actually likes your gender, so your chances may be nonexistent no matter what you say or when you say it. This is a good problem to have though, and it brings me right over to number three.

For the sake of argument, let's pretend that you have the attention of your object of affection. You should be ecstatic, but you have to keep your intentions a secret until the time is "right" or else you'll come off like an overexcited puppy that's about to piss on everything. You're expected to talk to the apple of your eye without telling them exactly why you are talking to them in the first place. Given, it may be fairly obvious that in order to talk to a stranger you must really find them attractive and want to go on a date, but maybe, *just maybe*, you really just wanted to be friends because that person had a cool shirt, or whatever the conversation starter may have been.

The point is, we have no way of knowing unless we say something to clarify our intentions. However, in this game that we have created, we are not allowed to say much of anything in the beginning. In our generation, showing interest in someone is equated with being clingy. We don't know how we deserve to be treated.

The area surrounding steps four through six is the exact location where every crevice of hell breaks loose. These steps have teamed up in order to screw all of us over. In this dating game, you have to hang out with the person whom you're interested in, but not ask them out too soon. In order to really raise the stakes, you must do this while you simultaneously keep yourself from being catapulted into dead man's land—better known as the friend zone. Please do not get me started on the part where you have to figure out how to best bring up the subject of dating to *ask* them on the stupid date. It's not an easy thing to incorporate into normal conversations. You know, now that you've spent some unspecified amount of time pretending to want to "just hang out."

I understand that we can't just spring these things on people, but it isn't like there's a chart to tell us when the time is right to suggest being more than friends. It may be a month, or it could be a year before the timing is exactly right. Every person is different with a different comfort level, so why is there so much societal pressure to get the timing right when everyone needs a different amount of time? I know no one has the answer to this, because like I said earlier, the shit doesn't make any sense.

I usually just get so frustrated with the stupid ass rules that I end up blurting it out at terrible times. That's *my* step seven. It is the time when shit goes completely out of my control, because this other person can say yes or no. The answer is usually no. In fact, the answer has *always* been no in my case. I've never won anyone over. I don't know why that is, and I'm not sure that I ever want to know the answer. All I know is that it has put me in the really awkward position of not knowing how to *actually* go on a date, which is step number eight.

What *is* a date, really? I get dressed in something other than sweatpants, and I'm assuming I meet this risk taker at the place that we decided to go. I mean, it's the twenty-first century. We don't have to ride there together do we? Anyway, we'll both get there, *somehow*, and then we just hang out? If that's all it is, then why the fuck don't we just call it hanging out? Seriously! What the hell am I supposed to do if I finally get a date? Explain that I've never been on a date? Wouldn't that raise a red flag? I think that would raise a red flag that I'm too weird to be datable.

"Hey Lucky Duck, I've never been on a date before, so you get to teach me how to date! Aren't you the dare devil?" Yeah, somehow I don't think that's going to work. I'm going to have to get a better plan.

Then there's the fact that we'd have to pay for stuff. Is it wrong to split the bill? Is it offensive? I'm not even sure anymore. The obvious solution to this would be to ask, but dating seems to be all about reading between the lines. I'm severely nearsighted. I can't see the damn lines!

There also seems to be vastly different rules about how many dates we're allowed to go on before we have to call ourselves a couple. Some people say that we should date one person at a time to show that we're serious. Other people think that dating only one person at a time makes us seem too clingy, so we need to date around to show that we have options and that our interest is true flattery.

I've also heard people claim that we need to date around to keep our options open, just in case we run into someone better. When is the cutoff point for this? Unless we become recluses we'll never stop meeting people, so do we avoid becoming part of a serious relationship in fear that we'll find someone "better?" I mean, no one is the best at everything, so technically everyone is better than someone else in someway. Oh God, I'm getting more confused as I type this.

I can't even get into the rules and ideas revolving around sex, mostly because I've never even gotten close to needing to know them. I don't understand it (societal rules, not sex). I don't understand why when we have the urge to do certain things with certain body parts of the people who make us tingle that it has to be such a taboo ordeal. It's not like any of us would be alive without it (unless you were an IVF baby).

I firmly believe that if we hadn't made it such a big deal, no one would feel the need to "lose it" at the exact "right" moment, or to lie in order to accomplish the task of getting into someone's pants. I think we'd all just experience it when we felt like we were ready, without regard to whether or not we're getting "too old" to still be virgins.

Virginity itself is confusing to me. I don't understand why it is referred to as "losing your virginity." Why is it considered a loss? I cannot think of any other situation in which we gain a new experience and it is considered a loss. That's just fucking depressing. Besides, if being a virgin is so important, then why isn't there a word for the opposite of virgin? Am I nothing once I'm not a virgin? I mean, at the rate I'm going, I'll probably never have this problem, but I'd still like to know the answer for reference purposes.

Anyway, let's just say that we manage to go on a date. From here, basically only one of two things are expected to happen. The first is that the date went poorly, and now we have to find a way never to talk to this other person again. There are no second chances and no friendships—all contact must cease because we aren't getting what we want. Isn't that mature of us?

The second outcome is that things go well. The next thing that I don't understand is that if the date goes well, why are we suddenly expected to be an instant couple? I mean, I guess with all of the waiting and guessing games played earlier, now everyone is in a rush to get the show on the road. Dating is viewed as something that we just do to burn up time—we don't know how much—before we either breakup or get married. (If you've noticed, step nine is to wait more, and I'm going to go ahead and guess that we'll need something to do while waiting to either breakup or get married, which is step ten.)

I think the problem with dating is that it's viewed as a step in an exclusive relationship instead of something to do when deciding whether or not a person is someone we'd like to *attempt* a relationship with. It essentially puts us into a situation where we are constantly, exclusively dating someone whom we just don't know that much about. If we spent half as much time dating as we do trying to get to the point where it was "okay" to ask someone on a date, then maybe the divorce rate wouldn't be at about 50%. This system sucks because half of the "successes" eventually fail. We constantly feel like we've wasted a bunch of time and emotion when a date goes badly. Well, that's probably because it took us eight months to get to that point. We DID waste a lot of time.

I'm not saying that I have all of these answers. Hell, I'm saying that I don't have *any* of the answers. I've never been on a date because I've never gotten the timing right with the right person. However, I've failed at it enough to know that something about this system is rigged, and it isn't rigged in anyone's favor. It is designed to make as many people as possible extremely confused. If things weren't this way, then there would be no good "reality" television drama, dating shows, sensationalized magazine articles, or dating coaches. (Seriously, what the fuck IS that?)

If I could make the rules, things would be very different. First of all, when we spot the person of interest, we'd go up and introduce ourselves. There wouldn't be a need to find an excuse to talk to them— we just *would*, and no one would think that it is a sign of desperation.

Step two would be to admit our intentions, but assure the other person that it's okay if the feelings are not returned—no pressure.

Step three would be to hang out, or what most people call "date." We'd be able to "date" more than one person at a time, because dating shouldn't be so serious. In my opinion, dating should be used as a tool to decide if we want to be in a relationship, not the sign *of* a relationship. It's too late at that point. We've already committed.

Step four would be to decide whether or not we like this person enough to be in a committed relationship. From this point on, it wouldn't be okay to "date" other people.

Step five would be the part where we'd just spend time together until we both decide to either break up or get married. That part will always be hard. That's a fact of life that no one can deny. Sometimes we'd both feel the same, sometimes we wouldn't, but at least we'd know where we stand, and we'd get there in a decent amount of time.

However, no one else seems to think that way, so unless you want to end up alone, you have to catapult yourself into those ten steps of hell. I, for one, do not have the patience for it. Until I meet another person who is as bullshit intolerant as I am, I'll just be alone. If being straightforward is something that I'm not allowed to do in dating, then dating is not something that I should spend my time trying to do, because I cannot read between lines. If I could, I'd probably be more socially accepted, but I'm not.

Sure, the curiosity is overwhelming at times. The loneliness can be equally as overwhelming at other times, but *most* of the time I feel okay. My need for less bullshit has always proven to be central to my mental well being, so I'm going to focus on that. I know that dating is expected of a young adult, and I know that I could be setting myself up to be more of an outcast than I already am, but I know how to deal with that stuff already. Sometimes in life we're lucky enough to get to pick the problems that we have. That opportunity doesn't come around often, but when it does, I'd suggest you exercise your right to choose. You'll find that some things are worth every bit of stress and heartache, and some things just aren't worth the trouble.

I've got better things to have panic attacks about than made up timeframes, and blind commitment. For me, dating is just not worth the trouble. I'll just have to find love by accident. It makes for a better story anyway.

-X

The Friend Zone

Being socially awkward automatically makes it harder for me to make friends, but it isn't a completely impossible endeavor. On the rare occasion when I meet someone who accepts me despite my limited knowledge of pop culture, tendency to talk too much, share too much, and rant for minutes at a time without stopping for air—then I tend to try to hold on to that person with every ounce of strength that I have. Obviously this human has just as many problems as I do, so we need to accompany each other through life's turbulent adventure.

In a world obsessed with money, fame, sex, status, and power, true friends are *ridiculously* hard to find. However, they're relatively easy to keep if you both accept each other on an "as is" condition. Contrarily, crushes are fairly easy to find, but they're *awfully* hard to keep because most of the time you two don't feel remotely the same way about each other. I think those are reasonably straightforward formulas to determine how much someone will complicate your life:

Friend = simple   Crush = confusing

However, the product of having a crush on a friend is *absolutely* the most agonizing ordeal that I've experienced in recent years, and keep in mind that includes my quarter life crises—all three of them. There is no formula in existence that can analyze this situation. It is a sloppy, disheveled, mind-constricting, panic-inducing, GMO of emotional turmoil, and I had the misfortune of experiencing it over a span of almost two fucking years. Yes, that's right, *two years*. I tried to move slowly because I was handling such priceless cargo.

Do you know the main difference between having a regular crush, and having a crush on a friend? When you have a regular crush, that's all that person ever was to you. If you lose them, then you lost your crush. That's honestly not such a big deal. Sure, your ego will hurt for a while, but you'll get over it. Crushes are easy to come by, remember? You'll have another one in no time. In fact, you may have had another crush at the same time that you were swooning over this crush. It's totally normal.

However, when you have a crush on a friend, that complicates shit. If you tell your friend how you feel and your friend doesn't return the feelings, then not only have you lost your crush, but there is approximately a 176% chance that you have just thoroughly fucked up your friendship beyond repair. True friends are hard to find, remember? You don't want to go 176% fucking up your friendships, but that's exactly what I did, because *I'm stupid*.

It started off innocently. I was just hanging out with my friend, just like any other day, then suddenly I'm having epic fantasies ranging anywhere from innocent dates out on the town, to full out banging on the kitchen table. I didn't know the definition of unsettling until I developed this crush, but I know it like the back of my hand now. I always felt like a kid who needed to be put into time out for "hiding" my feelings, because I felt like I was constantly lying even though I never explicitly lied about anything. However, I definitely got punished for my brain's misbehavior. I did two years of hard labor in the friend zone, and my release date wasn't exactly a cause for celebration, but I'll save that part for later.

I know I went on forever about crushes before, but this is like the crush psychosis on steroids. It is exceptionally easy to misread everything that a crush is doing, because it's human nature to want the people whom we like to like us back. I already know that what I hear in a conversation with a typical crush is the polar opposite of what that crush is actually saying. I'd be more surprised if I heard *anything* correctly instead of my own wishful thinking. However, when you're crushing on a friend there is affection there to begin with, so it is ten times easier to embellish all of those weird thoughts about whether something was a blink or a wink.

Besides, isn't it only natural to feel like you've found "the one" when you start crushing on a friend? I think that it is. If for no other reason, movies and music have recycled this theme so often that it almost feels unnatural to have a friend of the gender that you're attracted to, and not be attracted to that friend. I mean, shit, it's so common that it has even happened to me, and I've only had one *real* crush (and one casual one). What kind of fuckery is that?

There is no imagining that this crush feels more intense than a regular crush. How could it not? There are feelings invested by both parties…it's just that one party had a bit too much to drink, apparently. No, you're not fantasizing. Your crush *is* sharing secrets with you. Yes, you *are* hanging out a lot. Yes, your crush *is* texting you constantly. Yes! Yes! Yes! It's because you're *friends*! That's what friends do! Hopefully, you'll realize this long before I did, and keep your expectations ~~low~~ in check. I only pray that it isn't the moment after you've done something like try to stick your tongue down their throat—which thank *goodness* I have never possessed the kind of boldness that would have allowed me to try that.

It should be so easy to realize when you're being friend zoned, because you would think that you know your friend well enough to know how they would feel when they are receiving unwanted affection—even if you haven't known your friend for a very long time. NO! Everyone always seems to miss it until they are crushed by unmet expectations so many times that they start to find humor in it. Personally, I didn't know insanity until I was so deep in the friend zone that I actually wanted to forget what it felt like to have a friend.

You may find it surprising, but I've also done my fair share of friend zoning other people. It isn't fun. That's another reason why the friend zone sucks; it makes things awkward for *everyone* involved. No one wins when you're dealing with this thing. That's the one part about this whole fiasco that makes it so obvious that you two are friends—you're sharing the discomfort.

So, how do you know if you're in the friend zone? Well, ideally, you could just come clean about your feelings and find out from the person you're crushing on how they feel about you. Honesty is so underrated. Really, it is as simple as sitting down with your friend, explaining what is going on, and just getting it over with. However, we both know that none of us is going to try *that* shit until we're either binge eating, crying, extremely drunk, or all three of those at the same time.

I don't recommend any of those moments to come clean about this. I'm not an expert or anything, but as I've said, I have friend zoned a few people, and I've also been hairline deep in the friend zone. I've been on both sides of this electric fence, so I believe I learned a thing or two about this whole ordeal. I've experienced enough to know that honesty is the best policy, but that it is also the hardest act to practice. So, you can try looking for hints that your friend does not like the affection. You know, in case it isn't painfully obvious.

First, you have to realize that humans have instincts. A person will generally have a vague idea that you're crushing on them. Yes, even the socially awkward among you will know when someone is treating them a bit differently than the people who don't want to lick their face. What I'm trying to say is that your crush probably knows that you're crushing, and if that crush is your friend, then it's probably approximately 12.4 times more obvious than for a typical crush. It is also probably giving them all kinds of feelings of discomfort. If the conversations that you two share start leaving you feeling embarrassed instead of on that crush high, then you're in the friend zone.

There's nothing like trying to hang out with someone whom you have a crush on, and trying to assure them that you aren't attempting to trick them into a date. There's literally no way for you to ask your friend to hang out anymore without one of you feeling like you have a secret motive. That's why you'll start hanging out less, trust me.

In addition to hanging out less, I can bet my bottom dollar that you two will text each other a lot less than usual. Oh, who am I kidding? I'm a young adult. I don't have a dollar, but you can take my word for it. Even if by some slender chance in hell you two do keep up the regular texting, the conversations will be vastly different. They'll mostly consist of two uncomfortable people who are trying to pretend that the elephant in the room isn't taking a gigantic crap behind the couch.

When I told you about crushes, I said that your best friend probably gets just as excited as you do when you interact with the new love interest. That still holds true. So, if someone else comes clean about having a crush on you, and your friend basically does everything except kidnap you to sell you to that person, then guess where you're living? You reside in the capital of the friend zone.

If the crush that you have on your friend does not eventually pass on its own (which it won't because that would make life far too easy), then the truth *will* come out. One of you will eventually grow tired of feeling like you're walking on eggshells. Honestly, the sooner everything is out in the open the better. In fact, if you can avoid letting it get to this point, then do so. You can move on to damage control or a complete termination, either option will be less uncomfortable than being stuck in the friend zone.

I guess you're probably wondering what happened when I finally got released from my two year sentence. Well, I'm the festering type, apparently we both were. I let things fester until he could not stand it any longer, which was fine because I couldn't stand it either. However, to be completely honest with you, I didn't expect to *actually* have a conversation about it. I figured if it went on that long, then what was wrong with just staying that way? Obviously I wasn't going to make a move. I mean, I think two years was enough time to muster up courage if I had any (which I didn't). I didn't see the problem with letting things stay as they were because I wasn't interested in anyone else anyway. I wasn't missing out on anything. I couldn't lose the thing that I wanted because it wasn't mine to begin with. I'd already lost.

One night, soon after my birthday, I answered a phone call from him—which automatically made my voice go up approximately three octaves. (I really need to work on that hardware glitch.) Anyway, one tiny comment from me ended up being the gasoline to the fire. The next thing I know he's telling me to cut it out, and my ass is sitting on a metaphorical curb with no ride home. I know I'm nearsighted, but I did not see that shit coming. The solid proof in that was the fact that instead of doing damage control—like a normal person would do—I just spilled all two years of emotion out at once. I couldn't help it. I felt like a kid that got caught eating candy without paying for it, so I just freaked out and vomited all of the candy onto the floor. That only got me in more trouble, because now I was a thief and I also made a gigantic fucking mess on the floor.

The conversation ended with me saying that there was absolutely no obligation to speak to me anymore if I'd made things just far too weird. That invitation was not accepted, and for a while, I thought that maybe I'd escaped the 176% possibility of fucking up a friendship. However, it's been too many months for me count, and that's still the last conversation we had. Now, maybe I'm stupid. Maybe I really just cannot read between the lines when someone is just trying to be polite to me, but if I was going to lose anyway, then I would have liked to know just how badly I lost from the start. I constantly feel like something that was no one's fault is *my* fault, and there's no real way to fix that, because I can't make the discomfort just disappear. I made someone feel how other people make me feel every day. While I don't like the course of action, I fully understand it. I avoid interaction on the daily basis.

It is said that as we grow, the events that occur in our lives leave scars on us as a reminder of the tragedies we've survived and the lessons they taught us. If those scars were visible, there's no part of me would be left unmarked. My body would be a human memorial to clarity, simplicity, and flawlessness, but I still wish that I could see them because I know his mark would be the prettiest one. I could show the world the complicated web of pain and pleasure that etches upward from my stomach where the butterflies used to be, expands through the center of my chest where my heart ran races, and wraps around my throat where my words got stuck, until it lands right at the back of my mind where he remains. And honestly, I don't mind him being there. Beautiful artwork is worth the discomfort.

In all of those movies and songs that I mentioned earlier, only one of two outcomes occur. The first is that the two friends become lovers. The second is that they remain friends. My real life, not made for television, story ends with a third possibility. That's the one where you lose someone that you really care about and spend months feeling like a dumb ass.

You don't really know how to not feel like a dumb ass, because they never come back and explain their new decision. They never tell you what made them change their mind. They never tell you if that was the plan from the beginning and they just didn't know how to say it. Most of all, they *definitely* don't come back and tell you how you meant too much to them to sacrifice a friendship over something that was temporary and out of everyone's control. No, they just walk away without a word and never come back. *That's* the ending, which just so you know, doesn't feel like an ending at all.

-X

Hiding Elephants

I wonder if everyone can see
The tension between us two.
Our patience has grown so thin,
Surely our act is see through.
The smiles are painted on,
Like there's a cause for celebration.
But we both know something's wrong;
There's a crack in our foundation.
I have crossed a line,
Of which we dare not speak.
Comfort over honesty,
We keep our tongues inside our cheeks.
But if there's no spark between us,
Then there's nothing left to lose.
Communication has already crumbled,
There're no choices left to choose.
The truth is like a fire
Whose flames we've disavowed.
Everyone said we couldn't be friends,
Look at us proving it right now.
I can't comprehend,
Why we don't utter the truth to one another.
We can't even fake it for ourselves,
What makes us think we're hiding it from the others?
But you'll keep telling jokes,

Our friends will laugh and I'll assume,
That no one else but us
Is trying to hide the elephants in this room.

Kids (The Little Kind)

I'm old enough to remember the days when shows that practically glorify teenagers having babies were not in existence. I miss those days, because now babies are *all* I hear about! They're like the puppies of young adults. Everyone seems to want one, males and females alike. I know what you're thinking right now. It is probably along the lines of, "Kids? It's too early to talk about that! I'm not ready to be a parent! I can't even take care of myself!" That is probably true for most of us, but since I have the "luxury" of living in a conservative town, I've been getting bombarded by the topic of kids since I was about three years old.

I have nothing against babies. I do not think less of people who have them earlier than the average age of first time parents in the western world. However, I have a *huge* problem with being expected to want them, as though there is nothing else that I could possibly want out of life. It seems like people assume that every person who inhabits the planet was born solely to find another person so that they can have kids together.

Perhaps it is because I live in the South, but my first quarter life crisis—which I had much earlier than one would expect—included spending a week holding down panic attacks every time I saw a couple with a baby. It was like a subtle kick to the face to remind me that some people my age were already married and having babies, but I hadn't been on a date yet. This happened regardless of the fact that **I'm not even sure that I want kids,** *ever.* Nevertheless, society has done an excellent job of deeply instilling "baby panic" in 98% of the girls that I know, and at least 50% of the guys. Gender no longer makes you immune to the anxiety. That's when you know you're dealing with some heavy pressure.

When you're a little kid, you don't realize how much work you are to those around you. That isn't a negative thing; it's just a commonly accepted fact. I, for one, look back on myself as a child and I question how it is that my mom didn't ship me off to the circus, or at least just get up and run away from home. I further realized this when a couple of my classmates had babies at an early age. I watched vibrant, energetic teenagers become their version of the crypt keeper in a matter of months. If I hadn't questioned if I wanted kids before that, then I certainly questioned it after seeing how those tiny infants devoured their parents' souls in order to thrive.

Now, I'm by no means an expert in the baby-making business, but what I *do* have is a list of points that I have in response to the people who think that I'm batshit crazy for simply questioning whether or not I want kids someday. It is an attempt to bridge the gap; although I'm sure those who are in the midst of baby fever won't blink twice at the things that I mention here.

THE REASONS I QUESTION WHETHER OR NOT I WANT KIDS:

1. **They're *always* there.** For some people this is their favorite part, but there are those of us in the world who actually *enjoy* being alone. It isn't always lonely to be alone. In fact, I'd argue that it is healthy to be comfortable with having only yourself to keep you company. Most parents can't even pee alone, let alone have time to sit down to think. I have a timeframe of about three hours of interaction before I'm thinking of jumping out of cars, running away from home, or faking death in order to be alone. I don't know if I'm capable of adapting to having an optional, nearly conjoined human spawn with me at all times. People say that love conquers all, but I have my doubts.

2. **You have to be a *legit* grown-up.** This has absolutely nothing to do with chronological age. It's an evasive something else that I have yet to pinpoint, but I know for a fact that I don't have it. I don't know if I'm ever going to have it. It is hiding from me, and it is an expert ninja. If being an adult was a song, then I'm basically lip syncing twenty-

four hours a day, seven days a week, and I'm not even doing that great of a job.

3. **The unwanted advice will quadruple.** I get plenty of unwanted advice now, and I'm never quite sure of how to handle it. (I'm pretty sure that avoiding people is not handling the situation.) I don't even like when the automated machines give me instructions about how to operate it, so I cannot imagine how I'd handle someone telling me how to raise my kid.

4. **They're *FOREVER*.** This requires no explanation. YOU HAVE THEM *FOREVER*! (Well, by forever, I mean the rest of YOUR life. I know that this is assuming that your family is fortunate enough to avoid the tragedy of losing a kid, but the majority of kids in the US outlive their parents.) That's a very long, very scary period of time, and I do not suggest going into it without at least five minutes of serious thought. -_-

I could have gone into the age old explanation of the sleepless nights, poop explosions, and such, but in the words of my parents, "That's all temporary." Yes, they will grow up, but they are still your kids. You'll always have some sort of duty toward them, even if it's just an emotional one. The point that I'm trying to make is that kids are a permanent life change. It shouldn't be assumed that because I am human I cannot imagine a life without kids. I think it's absolutely dreadful to tell someone, "Your life isn't complete unless you have a kid." What if I cannot physically have children? What if the gender that I'm attracted to can't biologically make kids with me? Is my life forever incomplete because I didn't pass along my DNA? Seriously! Think about these things, and don't be an asshole by trying to plan other people's lives—especially if you don't know what circumstances they are battling.

The nerve of people when you bring up this issue never fails to amaze me. I mean, they're standing there telling me that one day I need to be a parent, but at the same time they don't think that I'm smart enough to make that decision without their help. Yes, raising a kid would be the *perfect* job for someone who isn't smart enough to realize whether or not they want one. What's more is that they insert the topic of kids into the conversation like it's *nothing*. "Oh, you need to have at least one kid."

If you don't believe me when I say that this whole statement is ridiculous, then I have a challenge for you. During your next conversation with your relatives, tell them that you want a tattoo—a *huge* one. I can almost promise you that the first thing out of their mouths will be something along the lines of, "Oh no! That's so *permanent*. It's so *expensive*. It'll make you less attractive to employers. You really need to think about this before you do it because you can't just get rid of it if you get sick of it."

Well…that's funny. That sounds an *awful* lot like having a kid if you ask me, but people have no problem telling us that we need to have a few of those little creatures.

I'm not saying that kids are life-ruining, terrible decisions. I'm not saying that I'll never want them. What I am saying is that in a time when most of us can't even find a job that allows us to pay rent without assistance from our parents or the government, maybe people should be a little more sensitive by not spewing at us how badly we need a kid or three. I'm sure there are plenty of people in the world who want kids, but cannot have them on their own. I'm sure there are even more people who want kids but cannot afford them. I mean, I wouldn't want kids just to have them, that's selfish. I'd want to be able to make sure they would stand a reasonable chance at having kick ass lives that are filled with things other than parents who are always at work, or childhoods spent not having their basic needs at all times.

Maybe it makes me crazy that I think so hard about these things (especially since my love life is about as active as a potato), but I can't help but feel like people are taking these things too lightly. It seems like everyone is having kids, but just because becoming a parent is *common* doesn't mean that it's *necessary*.

Parenting is literally having a human being's life dependent on your ability to be a teacher, chief, shrink, provider, and protector every second of every day, for the *rest* of your life. If you think I'm crazy for wanting a tattoo and for possibly not wanting kids, then I hope you're planning on seeing the shrink along with me, because you're crazy for thinking kids are a light matter. Permanence comes disguised in many ways. It's no one's place to criticize which of his aliases we choose to marry. I'm not saying that I'll never want kids, but I'm saying that until I get to a place where I can commit to something like a tattoo, then I should probably hold off on making other humans. After all, isn't that the responsible, adult thing to do?

-X

Toxic Relationships

Have you ever found yourself dreading a visit from someone? Have you ignored their text messages or hid their posts on social media? If your head or stomach starts to hurt in anticipation of seeing this person, even if you haven't nailed down a specific reasoning, you can bet your first born child that that person is toxic to you. Instinctively, you already know that you should distance yourself from that person, but being a part of this society you've been taught to believe that accepting the bad in others will make you a better person. Long story short, you put up with them because you've been told to accept people for who they are, even if that someone is an asshole.

Truth be told, dealing with other people's bullshit won't make you a better person. It'll make you cranky, miserable, and sometimes depressed, but not better. However, unless you are *extremely* lucky, then by the time you're a young adult you will have had the displeasure of having at least one toxic person in your life. If you're average, then you have probably had multiple toxic people in your life. I don't know when it became trendy to be a hardcore pessimist, but it needs to go out of style like loyalty and kindness did.

It should be noted that I'm not referring to genuinely depressed people here. That's an entirely different matter, and *that* needs to be taken very seriously. I'm referring to the people who look for problems just so that they can complain about them. They are the people around you who pretend that they have your best interests in mind, but are secretly (or maybe not so secretly) hoping that you fail. They are the people in your life who don't appreciate anything, no matter how amazing it may be. There is a meme floating around the Internet with an anonymous quote that says, "My mama always told me that they may want to see you do well, but never better than them." There is no word in the English language that I know of to express how true this statement has proven to be over the past few years of my life.

If you're (sort of) lucky, then there will be obvious signs that someone is a toxic person. They'll gossip about everyone, making sure to harp on any imperfection no matter how minor it is. They will be jealous of your accomplishments. They will insult you. Sometimes, they will "complisult" you—which is what I call a compliment with an insult attached to it. For example, if you hear something along the lines of, "Oh, congratulations on your new job! It was about time that you got a real one. I was getting worried," then that person just complisulted the *fuck* out of you. The "congratulations" that they gave you was about as genuine as a politician who's actively running for office.

If the person in question is obsessed with themselves, constantly insults others, flakes on most of your plans, but always expects you to come through for them—toxic! That human is toxic! The red flags are flying high, and you may want to reconsider whether or not you're okay with keeping that kind of negativity around you. (Hint: You shouldn't be.)

Unfortunately, identifying a toxic person can also be surprisingly difficult at times. When you're already feeling lost, confused, and unaccomplished, it feels natural to assume that you're the problem in any given situation. The disorientation that growing up can induce has a way of making you feel like if you've made one mistake, then you cannot trust anything else that you think anymore. *Obviously* your brain is broken and it gets everything wrong, so you're better off trusting a more "realistic" person. That's the term that I often hear when someone is describing a negative person: realistic. It is *really* realistic to believe that *everything* is inherently fucked up? I don't think that it is, so I don't view those people as being any more realistic than I do the people who think that everything is inherently perfect. As the old saying goes, the truth is somewhere in the middle.

If you're a creative person, then the amount of toxic people in your life, or at least the number of people who are toxic for you, is probably double that of a more "logical" person. You have the gift of being different, but different is often viewed as "childish" or "unrealistic" in our society. If you're not a doctor, lawyer, nurse, engineer, teacher, or (in some cases) an athlete, and if you're not striving to become one of those things, then your dreams have probably been attacked more than once before you even ate breakfast this morning.

Attacking creatively oriented dreams seems to have become a very popular thing to do in recent years. In fact, it is almost as trendy as complaining about everything and taking pride in being a toxic person. I cannot begin to tell you how many of my classmates would make fun of the amateur photographers in my school's photography club. WHY? Whom are they harming by taking really crappy pictures? It's not as if making fun of their dream will bring Toxic Tommy any closer to his own—if he even has one that means that much to him. Crushing another person's spirit serves no purpose, but toxic people do it as a hobby.

That's one of the most obvious characteristics of toxic people. They make fun of everyone else's dream. If they were focused on their own dreams, or at least on finding out what their dreams are, then there wouldn't be time to put anyone else's dream down. There is just no time for destroying other people's hopes and dreams when you're focused on your own shit. However, toxic people do this to distract themselves from the fact that they don't have that much going for them. The irony of it all is that it's at the toughest times of your life when you're most likely to attract toxic people because they will keep you around just so that they can watch you bathing in your misfortunes. It makes them feel better about themselves, now how is that for some fuckery?

The first time that I experienced a truly toxic person was a gigantic shock to me, because it was someone who I genuinely thought was my best friend. The story itself is fairly typical, but here it is: I knew that both school and office settings were not for me. (I cannot sit still for long periods of time.) I hate set schedules unless I'm setting the schedule. I hate not being able to make future plans because there's always overtime or call-in duties. I knew before ever setting foot into an office that those things were detrimental to my happiness. However, sometimes you have to do things that you don't want to do in order to get to where you want to be. It was during this time of finding a means to an end that I was the most miserable I'd ever been, ever—and I *went* to middle school, so this was some serious fucking misery.

One day near the beginning of my shift, I finally had enough. I found the guts to quit doing the thing that was making me unhappy, but instead of support, my "friend" told me that I "needed to grow up and deal with it." Some people say these things out of true concern for where your life is heading. Others say things like this because that is what they were taught the world should be like as an adult. However, in this case I'm 1000% sure that she was also miserable with her life. She didn't care about my well-being; she just wanted a more miserable person beside her so that she could feel better about herself. She and I are no longer friends, so that didn't quite work out in her favor.

To make things even more complicated, sometimes a toxic friend will pretend to support you full throttle, but as soon as you *really* need help for something they are missing in action. They don't answer your calls, texts, or respond to you on social media. They don't show up for any plans that you two made earlier. You actually begin to contemplate whether or not you should send a smoke signal to get in touch with them. That's because toxic people are never there when you need them. Despite what they may say to you, their actions will always show you their true feelings. When a person truly wants to be there for someone, it takes hell and high water to even try to stop them—but most of the time, it'll only make them a little late. If someone wants to be there for you, then they will find a way to be there, even if the only thing they can do is cry with you about how hopeless everything seems.

Toxic people also have a way of making you feel like you're a bad person when you don't feel like putting up with their shit. It is amazing to me how many times I've fallen into this trap—and I still do sometimes. There is a major difference between supporting someone and being their bitch. Supporting someone may come at three in the morning when life has crushed them, and they call you mid breakdown trying to locate a reason to get up and try again when the sun rises. Someone trying to make you their bitch is when no matter what you may have going on, they will call you every time the wind blows their hair the wrong way. They will get pissed off with you when you cannot come to their rescue for the 89th time that week, but won't think twice about what you'd have to neglect in order to be their lifeguard. Their only concern is what you can do for them.

Toxic people are not only found in friendships though, and that's where it gets increasingly tricky. Sometimes the people who are making you feel as though your soul wants to have lunch away from your body, just so you can get away from them, is *your family*. In the case of friendship, you have the power to choose not to be friends anymore. It may not be an easy thing to do, but you have the ability to revoke your friendship pass. You cannot undo the fact that someone is related to you. Your stage mom will always be your mom. Your overprotective dad will always be your dad. Your judgmental aunts will always be your aunts, and so on. You just cannot change those things. If you're really young, then you don't even have the power to control when you do or don't see them (which is yet another reason that childhood actually sucks, by the way).

Perhaps this is just based on personal experience, but I feel as though toxic family members are even worse than toxic "friends" because you are ingrained with the idea that your family is supposed to love you more than all of the other people on Earth, yet it's like they go for the jugular every single time you see each other. Their favorite topics tend to be: your body, your accomplishments, your sexuality, your religious beliefs, your political ideology, and your future plans.

There is no safe place to go with toxic people who have known you since birth. They can criticize you starting from a time when you didn't even know how to make spit bubbles, through every aspect of your entire life, until the present moment. In some cases, they'll even end their tirade by insulting the things that *you haven't even done yet*. I can't even with this. Can you? I definitely can't.

Many experts would suggest talking with this person to try to solve the problem, but here is the thing that they seem to forget—toxic people *never* think that they are toxic. They always assume that everyone else has the problem. If you try to talk to them about how they are treating you, then I guarantee you that the first words out of their mouth will be a statement that accuses you of being too sensitive or immature. Heaven knows that whatever the response is that they give you; it won't be any type of apology.

I guess it's only fair that I share how I ultimately handled my toxic relationships, and the answer is that I didn't. I just stopped replying to the things that those people said to me. I don't like conflict or fighting a losing battle, and that was a one way ticket to both of those hells. I started using the block feature on my phone. I blocked them on social media. I stopped hanging out with them—hell, at one point, I stopped opening the door. In the case of family, that's a work in progress. I often skip events. (Fun Fact: I'm skipping one now.) I leave the house when certain family members visit my parents. If I have to be in close quarters with them, then I just don't say much of anything. Basically, I just pretend that they don't exist, which doesn't solve the problem.

Does that make me a toxic person now that I make every encounter insanely uncomfortable? Maybe, but in true toxic fashion, I don't care. I'm happier. I don't worry about how bad my acne is, or if my body is at peak physical condition. I don't worry about the fact that I'm not dating anyone, or that I have no interest in anyone whom I'd have a chance at dating. I don't feel like I'm "wasting my life" just because I'm an introvert. I don't feel weird or selfish because I don't know whether or not I want kids someday. I especially don't feel half of the pressure that I used to feel over the fact that I haven't figured my life out yet. I'm aware that I cannot quit trying to progress into professional adulthood, but I also cannot just hit the clarity button and have it all figured out. These things take time, and time is something that toxic people are very stingy with.

We don't control time. We cannot always control when things happen for us, nor can we always control what happens to us. We *can* control what we give our attention to though. Fighting battles for our right to be ourselves is not one of the things that deserve our energy, so I, for one, have stopped giving it mine. I have better shit to do.

-X

Est. 199X

It is said that life can only be understood when viewed in reverse, but it has to be lived forward. I think that's true to an extent. There are things that have happened, and I only understood why it happened after everything else fell into place. Other times, I find that no matter how hard I try I cannot figure out the reason something had to happen. Yes, everything happens for a reason, but sometimes that reason is because shit happens.

I could blog all day long, but I'll never be able to reach the person who needs to hear these words the most—my 12-year-old self. I wish I had the ability to write a letter to my younger self, so that I could help myself avoid years of worry, heartache, and other wasted emotion. However, since I cannot time travel, I'll share the letter with you. You know, just in case you're a kid who stumbled upon this stuff. The advice that I have to offer may not apply to you, and if it doesn't, then don't apply it to yourself. As I've said, this is just what I wish I could go back and tell myself when I was a child. You are under no obligation to understand.

Little X,

By now you have probably figured out that the world that you live in is both too big and too small. On one hand, there are so many options for you to choose from, so many things to succeed or fail at, that you often don't know where to go. On the other hand, it seems like no matter where you go you cannot escape the problems that plague you anyway. Some days it feels as though you've tried everything there is to try to solve your problems, and you still haven't found any solutions. Don't worry; that's a perfectly normal feeling. Just about everyone feels like that at some point in their life, but no one ever really admits it or tells us how to deal with it. Now, while I don't know everything, I do have some very important advice that I'd like to rush deliver to you so that maybe you can ease into young adulthood a little bit more smoothly than you're currently set to do.

The first thing you need to know is that everything that seems like a big deal now will *not* seem like a big deal in the future. It's not that your parents don't care about what's going on in your life, it's just that 98% of it— no matter how huge it seems now— will not matter to you in a year. The item that you think you HAVE to have isn't nearly as important as making sure that a household is up and running. Money is hard to come by, despite how easy it seems. Give your parents a little break, their lives are harder than you think they are, but you won't be able to possibly comprehend that until you're trying to do it yourself. You just have to take my word for it.

Second, popularity is bullshit. You *think* that you have conflicting desires by having social anxiety but also wanting to be popular, but popularity isn't what you really want. What you're craving is to feel accepted. Just so you know, popularity is *not* when everybody loves you. Popularity is when everybody *pretends* to love you. You'll barely find a real friend in the bunch, if you find one at all. The people who are still remaining when you need someone will never be the people you expect it to be. Also, as obvious as this seems, I cannot repeat it enough: **Do not trust everyone.** People will tell you *anything* to get what they want from you. If you really want to see the type of person someone is, then observe how they treat someone who can't do anything for them. That's how they will treat you when you need help.

That brings me to my next point, which is that sooner or later, *everyone* needs help. It does not matter how old you are. It does not matter how much money you have (or don't have). It does not matter how many awesome things you have achieved. As humans, sometimes we need another human. It doesn't have to be a financial need either. Sometimes life gets emotionally taxing, and you will just feel like a failure at everything. Hell, even if you *are* successful sometimes you'll feel like you faked your way there.

That's when you'll really need someone, because you're probably about to have some type of life crisis. (You have those a lot.)

I know you feel as if everyone has their life in perfect order except for you, but it helps if you remember that people are just like bedrooms. What I mean is that just because it looks like everything is perfect on the outside doesn't mean that there isn't a pile of shit stuffed in the closet or hiding underneath the bed. You need to be considerate of the things that other people are not telling you—which is a skill that a lot of adults don't bother to pick up, but you'll be happier once you do. Not only will it allow you to feel more comfortable with your progress in life, but it'll also help you to accept apologies that you deserve but never receive. Your peace is more important than your pride. People will mistreat you, break promises, and step on you to get where they want to be in life, and they'll never apologize for it. There is no use in harboring that anger or campaigning for an apology that wouldn't be sincere anyway. Let them get away with it, but never let them do it again.

As you grow up, you'll start to realize that surviving and achieving success in this world isn't about *what* you know as much as it is about *whom* you know. It's unfair, I know, but that's the reality of the world that you live in. That's why people try so hard to make other people like them. The pressure to fit in or to impress others will always be there, and no matter what you do there will *always* be a way for you to fit in better, at least according to society. I know you think that if you try hard enough to make people like you, then they will. I hate to break it to you, but they won't. It is best to just let go of that shit early on, that way you won't waste time trying to remember who you are because you forgot while you were pretending to be someone you weren't.

The good news is that your success only depends on those people if you're trying to get the success from them (like a job). Forget about the part where you try to come across as a worthy employee, because you're just not good at it. Instead, spend your time trying to figure out how to become the person whom other people are trying to impress. The window of opportunity gets jammed sometimes. When it doesn't open for you, pick something up, throw it as hard as you can, and shatter the fucking glass. What I'm trying to say is that you're one of those people who'll have to create your own opportunities; no one is going to give them to you. You're better off finding a skill that you love and are proficient in, and just running with it while hoping for the best.

That being said, you also have to learn the art of being flexible enough to adapt when things don't go according to plan. I like to call this being able to flux and flow, but you can call it "being adaptable" like other boring people if you want to. The hatred that you harbor for five-year plans seem like a trait of irresponsibility to the professional adults in your life, but trust me, it stems from an internal instinct that is telling you that those plans lead to your destruction.

You're too much of a perfectionist to make a plan and not have it work out *exactly* the way you planned it. Some people blame that on your anxiety issue. That's not your anxiety; that's your human side being human. If you can come to the future and find five people who like to have their plans fall through, then I'll eat those words with a moderate dose of Xanax. The fact is that you cannot plan for five years into the future. You aren't psychic, for fuck's sake. Go with your instincts and tell the five-year plans to fuck off.

However, not planning five years into the future does not mean that you get to neglect thinking about your future. You cannot just blow things off and expect it all to work out at the last minute. That's why you have to learn the art of balance. Try to get a basic idea of what you want, then look for ways that you can inch closer to achieving that goal. You do not have to stress about which dream is the "right" one while in this process if you don't already know what it is. You can make a list of the dreams that seem appealing to you, and then try them all. The one that ends up working, if any, was the right one.

Also, choose your dreams based on pleasure, work-life balance, and ability; *not* profit, status, and stability. I know what you're thinking. What's wrong with stability? Nothing, except that *it doesn't exist*. Sure, there are some jobs that are more abundant than other jobs, but that doesn't mean that you'll get chosen for any of them. (There's the part where you have to impress people, remember?) It also doesn't mean that the next big invention won't happen and you'll be out of a job. It means that those jobs are reliable right now, but you have to live beyond right now (You just can't think about it too much or you'll go into tizzies and shit).

This is probably the most important thing I can tell you: **Do not stress out about school**. School doesn't really control much in the "real world." (No part of the world or your life is fake, FYI.) Instead, learn a few skills. That will be useful in a work setting. You *may* even be able to get a job. I don't know why it works this way, but it does. I'm not sure what school is there for now, but employers like skills and work experience more. Get those instead of going insane to get that 4.0 GPA that you were proud of for all of about a week. One week of pride versus the ability to land a job...you pick, but your future self would *really* like a job.

I know you don't have friends right now, but it's not a lost cause. Stop beating yourself up, and be a little more patient. There will be people in your life who affect you so deeply that you can light up a stadium with the sparks you feel while with them. It's absolutely beautiful, just wait for it. Word of advice though, don't hold back with how you feel. One day, you'll wish with every fiber of your being that you had told someone very special just how special they were. Let's leave it at that for now.

As for love, I really wish that I could tell you that you got better at that whole dating thing, but you didn't. In fact, you may have gotten worse seeing how there is a growing list of people who have turned you down. Don't stress out about your first date, first kiss, or first relationship, because as of my time, none of that has happened yet anyway. The important thing to remember is to never get so desperate or impatient that you end up settling for less than you deserve. It's better to be single than to be with the wrong person. I can't tell you how to change this trend, but the good news is that you genuinely won't care nearly as much. Actually, you become more reclusive to the point where you don't really crave it at all anymore.

However, every blue moon someone will come along and make you feel *a lot* of things. Fuck the dating rules, tell that person how you feel about them right from the beginning. That way if things have to fall apart, you didn't waste a bunch of time, energy, and emotion on someone who simply did not feel the same way about you. In the end, the emotional investment results in a deeper cut than the realization that it will never happen. You cannot control who rejects you, but you *can* control how long you spend letting them warm up for the occasion. Procrastinating about it won't change the answer, and you'll always miss your time more than you miss that person, trust me.

Oh, and speaking of being rejected, that's okay too. Rejection is actually *not* the end of the world. It doesn't mean that something is wrong with you. It doesn't mean that you did anything wrong. It just means that two people didn't feel the same way about each other. That's really all it means. You'll be better off if you learn this sooner rather than later.

Finally, your future self wants you to know that your struggles are not exclusive to anxiety disorders. The fears you have are as common as a five-year plan (though you may react to them a little more intensely than some people). Someone out there will understand if you give them the chance. Growing up is confusing, stressful, and panic-inducing, but so is being human. No one is supposed to feel comfortable ALL the time; negative feelings are just a part of life. You felt all of those things before someone considered you an adult, and you'll feel it afterward.

I know you spent almost your entire life up until now being told that you have to work to establish yourself. You're being told that you have to figure out who you are, and then prove to the world that you're as great as you think you are. The truth is that you were *born* established. We all are. You don't have to try to make yourself worth something because you're already priceless, and fuck anyone who doesn't see it. It is not your job to prove to anyone that you're a worthy of good things. You have to know that for yourself. You aren't going to find that worth in money. You won't find that in material objects. You won't find it in anything that you arrived to this life without. You didn't need it to be someone then, and you don't need it now. If your worth is being determined by something that is outside of yourself, then you're being shortchanged.

You will enjoy yourself a lot more if you remember two things about how to face the challenges in life. The first one is to try, and the second one is to *keep* trying. That may sound a little daunting or depressing, but it is actually pretty good news for someone who is terrified of the idea of becoming an adult who is stuck in monotony, because then you may realize that no one ever reaches a place where they are "stuck" being one thing. You literally grow every single day that you are alive. You only stop when you're dead, or when you choose to stop trying. If you're not dead, then that means that you still have a chance to learn something new and make your life a little more interesting than it was yesterday. Even if you're failing at the thing that you are trying, you're still learning from mistakes that you haven't made in the past. You're still getting the chance to do new things.

What I'm trying to say is that growing up doesn't mean that the fun is over. It means that you get to choose whether or not you have fun. The perks of being an adult aren't hard to find. You get to make your own choices. You hold a bigger influence in society. You have a better idea of what works for you and what doesn't. You can decide whom to keep beside you, and whom to let go. You become better at spotting people who don't have your best interest at heart. The things that used to destroy you aren't strong enough to do so anymore. There are a *lot* of perks to growing up, but the *best* part is when you realize that you don't have to wait for someone to give you a gold star. You're an adult now, and your life belongs to you. You don't need anyone's permission anymore. You can just reach out and take one.

-X

Young Adulthood Glossary

Alcohol - A decently expensive beverage that young adults can't afford, but always seem to have in excess.

Bills - Depression in paper form.

College - The location of a mythical fortune that attracts thousands of young adults to its doors each year. Entry fees range from $0 to $250,000+ per four month visitation.

Complisult - A compliment that is attached to an insult. The insult is the dominant intention in this situation.

Confusion - A young adult's seemingly permanent state of being.

Crushlationship - A relationship in which the object of affection does not know that they are dating their admirer.

Five-Year Plan - A mythical idea that we can control every aspect of our lives so well that we can foresee every event for the next five years.

Friend Zone, The - The area where someone with misplaced romantic feelings awkwardly resides immediately before completely ruining a friendship.

Gap, The - The phenomenon in which two people of the exact same age could be living two totally opposite lives, but neither of them seem completely appropriate or inappropriate for their chronological age.

Job Application - A sheet of paper which gives employers the information needed to tell you that you are both overqualified and too inexperienced.

Job Hunting - The process of seeking out rejection.

Job Interview - An event when a hiring manager verbally asks you all of the questions that you answered on the job application.

Money - Something young adults desperately want and need, but never seem to have in their possession.

Professional Adult - An adult who has survived their quarter life crisis and tends to have more organization in their life than ten young adults combined.

Quarter Life Crisis* - The time during which you only understand about 3% of your life, and time suddenly accelerates to a speed greater than light or sound.
*May occur well before age 25

Real Job - The mysterious job title that no one ever seems to hold. Studies suggest that the "real" job is one that is outside of the retail, food, janitorial, and other blue-collar service areas. It must pay enough money so that its holder can purchase everything they are told that they need, which is not to be confused with what they *actually* need. In some cases this job requires heavy lifting to display work. In other cases, this must be a desk job to prove status. More research is underway to conclude a more specific definition.

Social Media* - A digital community in which employers stalk their employees with the sole purpose of finding reasons to fire them—despite the fact that these reasons were never a problem in the workplace.
*Also a place where embarrassing photos are posted, people are suddenly very open about depression and/or complaints, and everyone becomes a political expert.

Student Loans - Very expensive reminders of our poor life choices.

Struggle Steaks - The term coined by Gary Washington to describe the steak-like substance sold at various dollar stores in the US.

Young Adult - Someone who understands 6% of their life or less at any given point in time.

About the Author

Ki Etienne is a '90's Kid who enjoys fitness, cartoons, video games, the Internet, being a Nerdfighter, reading, writing (obviously), and a good stir-fry. She currently lives in Louisiana with her parents and overweight dog. No, she does not plan on changing that any time soon. :)

She would love if you visited her at one of her lovely cyber homes:

Twitter: www.Twitter.com/LOCKnKiii
YouTube: www.YouTube.com/LOCKnKiii
Goodreads: www.Goodreads.com/LOCKnKiii
Tumblr: www.LOCKnKiii.tumblr.com

The blog dedicated to this novel can be found at:
www.established199X.tumblr.com

www.ingramcontent.com/pod-product-compliance
Lightning Source LLC
Chambersburg PA
CBHW071129200626
46817CB00018B/2492